Disco
Fever

To Sophie

Disco Fever

E.B. Hawkins

With best wishes

E. B. Hawkins

SIMON &
SCHUSTER

SIMON &
SCHUSTER

First published in Great Britain by Simon & Schuster UK Ltd, 2004
A Viacom company

1 3 5 7 9 10 8 6 4 2

Simon & Schuster UK Ltd
Africa House
64–78 Kingsway
London WC2B 6AH

A CIP catalogue record for this book is available from
the British Library

ISBN 0689837550

Typset by SX Composing DTP, Rayleigh, Essex
Printed and bound in Great Britain.

To Edward

Warning

I'm not brilliant at writing and you don't know my friends, so to keep it clear, here's the score.

My Mates.

My best mates

Josh – sophisticated, snappy dresser, knows it all
Connor – a technical genius, my oldest and frankly most embarrassing friend

My other mates

Harry – stinking rich
Adam – Harry's sidekick, tough and not a mate to get on the wrong side of

My room-mate

James – my little brother and tormentor

Then there's **Zoe**, **Amanda** and **Stephanie**. They're not mates – they're girls. Not forgetting my big cousin **Amy**, she's annoying.

Finally there's me, **Matthew Evans**, and to find out what my mates and I did about the disco, you'll have to read on . . .

One

Eleventh week of the winter term. The weekly meeting of Year Seven of St David's School for Boys. That was when the bombshell landed.

There must have been about a hundred of us, the three classes of the first year of St David's, lolling on the seating tiers of the school hall. We gazed down at the balding pink pate of Mr Grinston, which was criss-crossed with a few stringy strands of hair.

'Your attention, boys. First the bad news . . . Adam, yes, I *am* talking to you. Remove your feet from the chair in front of you! In ten days' time we have end of term tests in maths, English, science, French, technology, geography and history.'

That woke us from our stupor.

'What?'

'Sir, that's evil, that is!'

'We can't revise a whole term's work!'

'It's against our rights,' I yelled in the growing din.

Mr Grinston's head sank to his chest so that the lights glistened on his bald patch. Then slowly he looked up, revealing a smile as tight as an elastic band.

He held his hand up for quiet.

The shouting dwindled as we saw he wasn't in the least put out by our protests. A last lobbed 'It's not fair, sir!' hung in the air before it fizzled out.

'But, boys, life is not fair,' smirked Mr Grinston, lowering his hand. 'And the sooner you learn it the better.'

He was right, life certainly is unfair. Last year, Mr Temple, the new science master and football coach, was head of Year Seven, and I bet Mr Temple wasn't even born when old Grinston started teaching at St David's. Mr Temple is a laugh, good fun. One look at Grinston and you feel seriously depressed.

'These tests should be no problem to most of you,' Mr Grinston droned on. 'If you have kept up with your work, and most of you have, they will not be difficult. They are merely to help us decide which groups would be best for you when we begin setting next term.'

We sat in stunned silence. Sets, that's when they decide whether you have any brains or not.

'Now the good news,' said Mr Grinston, and the elastic band across his face stretched fit to burst.

His eyes rose up to the tiers in front of him, drifting

and lingering over us, wallowing in the rare attention he was getting.

'There is usually some small end of term celebration for the first years. This year I have decided we will try something new: a Christmas disco.'

I wasn't sure I could believe what I'd heard. Connor nudged me.

'Yeah, a disco,' I said.

Connor blinked.

A disco?

How could old Grinston, with what remained of his grizzled hair curling ridiculously long about his ears, in his droopy blue jacket and faded brown cords, even know what a disco was?

His grin faltered as he faced his shocked audience. It took a lot to shut us lot up.

'The last Friday of term. Something to look forward to when the tests are over. The head and I are concerned that when you boys come to St David's you lose touch with those good friends of your primary years who have moved on to St Anne's.'

'What's he going on about?' Connor whispered loudly on my left. 'My friends are all here.'

'Girls!' Josh enlightened us from the right.

'Yeah, that's right,' I said, remembering. 'Zoe, who used to pinch our ball and hide it, and that swot Stephanie, who always wanted to help us because she got all her maths right.'

'And Amanda, who destroyed my spaghetti bridge,

which I took weeks to make, because she said she thought it was for her food project.'

'It didn't look much like a bridge,' I ventured.

'Course it didn't, Matthew,' said Connor. 'It was ahead of its time. A new suspension system. Could have made me a fortune.'

'They're all at St Anne's now.'

'Who are?'

'The girls, stupid.'

As the news sank in, the chattering grew and grew.

'The head and I are concerned that you continue friendly contact with St Anne's and we hope in due course to arrange a joint music, drama and art appreciation society for first years. We are tied to single-sex secondary schools by the provisions of our church founders, but that is no reason why we shouldn't join forces in areas of mutual interest.'

Sniggers broke out further along our row from where Adam was sitting. Then behind me gusts of raucous laughter exploded. Connor, Josh and I looked at each other and then joined in too.

I caught up with Josh on the way back to the classroom.

'What do you make of that, Josh?'

Josh stared ahead, then shrugged his shoulders. He wears these designer specs which fade from light to dark in bright light, so it looks as if he's wearing dark glasses. They're impressive. His two grown-up brothers joined together to buy them for his birthday. The trouble is, because I can't see his eyes I can never tell what he's thinking.

'What's the shrug mean?'

'Tests, nobody bothers about tests,' he said lazily, running his fingers through his dark hair. It's meant to stick up. I wish Mum would let me have a haircut like that.

Josh was lying of course. We all say that, and that we don't do any homework and that we're not bothered, but there's always a pile of work sitting on the teacher's desk when they ask for it.

'I was meaning about the disco,' I added.

'Oh, the disco.' Josh chuckled, as if he'd cottoned on to some private joke. 'My brothers used to go to discos. They go to clubs now.'

I wasn't sure what that was supposed to mean. Did Josh go to discos too? He obviously knew a lot more about discos than I did.

I don't know too much about Josh. He wasn't at our primary school, but we have desks behind each other in class and he knows a lot of stuff I don't. I bring my work to school in an old sports bag, but he carries a special black bag that was his brother's, with a space on the strap for a mobile phone, only he's lost the phone.

Josh is taller than me, lanky, with a ghostly pale face, dark eyes when he takes his designer specs off and black hair.

'Interesting-looking boy,' Mum says.

Not that I remember Josh saying anything interesting

this term, but nobody says 'interesting-looking boy' about me. Still, Josh is all right and I was secretly surprised he actually wanted to be friends with me.

Connor caught us up from behind.

'Do you think our projects will count in technology?' he panted. 'I've still got the wheel uplift on my suspension system to work out. We're meant to be going to Gran's on Sunday, but Mum might let me stay at home to finish it.'

Oh, Connor!

My best friend through nursery and primary school, Connor is always building and inventing and designing. Just like his dad. It was fun when we were little. Connor could always work out how to make a tree house or build a Lego space model so big I had to climb over it to get into bed. Connor's always got some plan, some project he's mad about.

But Connor couldn't care less whether his crinkly ginger hair stands up or flops over, and as his tattered old school bag is usually being used to store something he's making, he brings his homework to school in a Tesco plastic bag.

Connor thinks that because we've always been mates we always will be. He was embarrassing with Josh around. Not that Josh had said anything yet.

'Who cares about our projects!' I said. 'So what's up with the disco, Connor?' and I tried a Josh–style chuckle, but it came out squeaky.

Connor stood still and blinked.

'Well . . .' he said at last. 'If it's going to be in the gym the lighting is useless.' He stared intently at the floor and I knew his brain cells were powering into action. 'You know that *Top of the Pops* on telly, my sisters watch it . . . all flashing, coloured lights. We'll need some of those. I'll ask Mr Grinston what he's planning, because I've got a few ideas for a lighting circuit . . .'

You see what I mean?

Two

All through the rest of the day it went like this:

'What do you think of this disco rubbish?'

'Grinston's off his rocker. He's making a pathetic attempt to be popular.'

'Are you going?'

'Dunno . . . are you?'

'I might.'

I knew I would be going whether I liked it or not. Mum has this thing about joining in school activities. She says, 'You never know if you like something until you've tried it.' She always wants me to be sociable. Her dream come true would be to have me voted the Most Popular, Most Hard-working Wonder Boy of St David's.

It won't happen in a million years. But Mum can't bear the thought that a son of hers isn't going to turn out the dream child she feels she's entitled to after all her 'hard work'.

Josh had brought in a new packet of crisps for his lunch. They were prawn and won ton sauce flavour, bright pink with tiny brown speckles. I swapped him two of my beef and mustard, and then Connor muscled in and offered two pathetic ready-salted crisps.

'Mum bought this good-value bulk buy at Ready Save,' he explained. 'We didn't discover they were plain until we got home.'

Josh took pity on him and held out his silver prawn and won ton crisp bag, and he didn't even watch as Connor plunged his hand in.

'Thanks, Josh!' Connor grinned. 'Help yourself to mine.'

I'd have watched Connor like a hawk, or else I'd have counted out just two crisps. But Josh isn't bothered.

Then I remembered . . . It was crisps that made us mates in the first place. Josh and I sat next to each other in the canteen the first week of term and we had this conversation about whether you can taste the difference between cheese and onion crisps and cheese and chive. So we had a blind tasting and we both got it right.

We're experts on crisps. After school we spend ages at Mr Patel's shop on Elgin Road, choosing which crisps we're going to spend our pocket money on.

'Ugh!' said Connor. 'Disgusting! You can keep this won ton rubbish.' He held out two prawn and won ton crisps. 'I'll have my plain ones back.'

Josh tipped his chair so that it balanced on its back legs and sighed.

'Eaten them,' he said.

That's Connor . . . no sophistication. Prefers plain crisps.

'Mr Grinston said I can design a circuit for some proper lighting,' Connor said, spitting out bits of ham roll from his packed lunch as he talked. 'We thought red, orange and green, like the traffic lights. I bet my dad will help.'

'What for?' I pretended not to know.

'The disco, of course.' Connor blinked, and then took another mammoth bite of his ham roll.

'You're going, then?' I said casually.

'Course I am. It'll be great, with red lights from the corners and green from the ceiling . . . You lot must be coming.'

Josh smiled lazily, as if Connor was a right joke.

'There'll be girls,' Josh muttered. 'Big deal!'

'Wow!' I said, to show I didn't care about girls either.

Then I choked. They can overdo the mustard on beef and mustard crisps.

It was the same about the tests. I'm quite good at maths, but I can never think of anything to write in English when I'm meant to be creative. I mean, we can't all be Shakespeare or Charles Dickens. Some of us will have to do real work when we grow up, so what's the point of writing 'An Imaginary Shipwreck on a Desert

Island'. The only island I've been to is Brownsea Island, in Poole harbour, and they've got a great café there and a little beach from which you can spot the TruckLine cargo ship coming in every afternoon with lorries from France.

And French. That's another nightmare. It goes in one ear and out the other. After English, it's my worst subject.

Mum says that when I grow up, everyone who wants a job with lots of money will have to speak another language. So if I'm no good at English and no good at French, I'm done for.

At three-thirty Connor, Josh and I headed out of the school gates. December and it was already getting dark, with the wind buffeting down Elgin Road in icy gusts. My hands were frozen, but I didn't take my woolly gloves out of my pocket because Josh never wears gloves.

Harry was leaning against the gates, his hands deep in black gloves up to his elbow, like motor-cycle gauntlets, only he says they're for skiing. Adam, his sidekick, was waiting beside him, his nose blue and his eyes watery with cold, but Adam's cold because he's got a number one and so little hair it's like stubble.

'Who cares about the tests?' Adam was saying. 'I'm not doing any extra work. Grinston should have told us earlier.'

'Actually,' said Harry, tossing back a strand of his

shiny blond hair, 'my dad bought me some revision CDs when he was in New York on a business trip. They're the latest technology, not available here. You set the CDs to play when you're asleep. The information is absorbed by your brain and ... guess what? It's sunk in when you wake up in the morning.'

Connor pushed forward and stared at him.

'Harry, how's that going to work? I mean, the CD gabbling on all night, it'll keep you awake and then you won't learn anything.'

We gathered round Harry to listen.

'*No*, Connor, there is *no* noise.' Harry smiled down at Connor, who's a bit on the short side. 'The CDs play subliminally, below the sound of human hearing.'

We all stood there gazing at Harry. And I know what we were thinking.

Harry Seymour is so stinking rich, it's unfair. It's unjust.

Or is it?

We had some fantastic birthday parties at his house when we were at the primary school, with paid entertainers and special caterers and loads of party gifts. We went completely wild, chucking peanuts and ice cream and cake at each other, because Harry's mother only appeared at the end, when all the other parents arrived.

So Harry being stinking rich is unfair but OK if we get a look in on it.

'Harry,' I said, trying to sound friendly but not too

cosy, 'have you got a French CD? I mean . . . I wonder if I could borrow . . .'

He dazzled me with his white-teeth smile.

'I'll be using mine, Matthew,' he said. 'But I'll ask my dad to e-mail New York tonight and we'll get you your own.'

'What'll that cost?'

'Don't worry. Money's no problem if you know where to look.'

I fingered the three coins in my pocket. I knew I had enough for a Coke and some barbecued sausage-flavoured crisps on the way home, and a garlic chicken packet tomorrow, but then I was skint. No more pocket money till Saturday.

'On second thoughts, Harry, I'll stick with our book.'

Harry climbed into the all-terrain Explorer Jeep driven by the latest in the army of au pairs who looked after him. Adam leapt in behind him and grinned and waved out of the back window to us, as the au pair, a big girl with long droopy hair, accelerated away.

'Creep!' I said.

Connor, Josh and I headed for Mr Patel's.

'They've been conned,' said Connor, blinking. 'They must have been. If the human ear can't hear anything, how is the information on the CD going to be transmitted to the brain.'

That made me feel a bit better. But not much.

Because what I have been trying to tell you all this time is that I was worried. Dead worried.

With lousy test scores, I'd go into lousy sets, then I'd do lousy exams and, when I finished school, I'd get a lousy job. All this 'doing well' Mum goes on about is like a long chain and the first link is the first year at St David's, or so she says.

And then there was the disco. I couldn't dance. I've never had a sense of rhythm or been able to hear 'the beat' in music.

I wouldn't mind seeing Zoe and Amanda again, but if I went to the disco I'd only make a fool of myself.

I'm a worrier. I've always been a worrier, and it was getting worse.

Three

The ten days that followed were BAD.

Mr Grinston announced that the tests would be staggered and that science was first. Every evening after school I was up in my bedroom, fighting off my little brother, James, who wanted me to help him play games on our computer.

'Just leave me alone, will you?' I said. 'Can't you see I'm trying to work?'

He tried to pounce on me, diving off his bunk onto my desk.

'Cut it out,' I yelled.

It's about time he grew up. He's started in the second year in primary school now. We used to roll around playing tigers on the floor, at least I was Big Tiger and he was Baby Tiger, and he still thinks he's little enough for that sort of thing. But I'm too old now and it's irritating that he hasn't got the message.

I was just reading about why ships float. It's because they are not as dense as water. Most ships are made up of metal wrapped round lots of air, what with the cabins and cargo holds and engine rooms, so most of the volume of the ship is air and less dense than water. Interestingly, the *Titanic* had a . . .

'No . . . I am *not* going to play with you. Go on . . . Give me that game. No, you can't have it. Why not? Because I'm working for a big science test.'

James stared at me as if I was mad and then ran out of the bedroom.

'Waah! Waah! Matthew's taken my game. He's horrible.'

Dad was downstairs in the kitchen. On the days Mum works full-time, Dad starts and gets back early. Other days Mum comes home early.

'Horrible, is he?' I could hear Dad's rumble.

Dad has a way of always repeating what you say, as if he's heard but hasn't really. It's just the robot inside answering while he has a rest.

'He won't play with me . . . Waah! Waah!'

'Won't play with you . . .'

I could hear James working himself up into a state. He often does this after school.

A key rattled in the lock downstairs and the front door slammed.

'What's going on in here?' Mum called as she headed

down the passage for the kitchen. 'That child is tired. What he needs is some food and a story.'

'Food and a story,' said Dad, as if it was a mystery solved.

Bump! went Mum's bag on the kitchen floor.

'Look at that, Simon. The rubbish bucket is overflowing. Didn't you think to empty it?'

'Rubbish bucket?'

'It really is too bad to come home to this mayhem. I'm working the same hours you are now, Simon. A modern marriage, that's what we said we were going to have. Share the work and share the chores at home. And what greets my tired eyes as soon as I put a foot over the threshold? Screaming children and overflowing rubbish.'

'Excuse me,' I said as I walked into the kitchen. 'If you lot kept your voices down I could do some work.'

'Work!' screamed Mum. 'You don't know what work is.'

She stared at me with wild eyes.

If James was tired, Mum looked exhausted, with dark patches under her blue eyes. Her eyes are the best bit about her and they used to laugh and sort of twinkle before she went back to work full-time.

'I am revising for my end of term tests.'

'End of term tests,' said Dad, tying an apron round his waist. 'You'll be all right. That's why we got you into a good school like St David's. It wasn't easy, living outside the catchment area.'

'But if I don't get decent marks I won't get into good

sets and then I won't do well in exams and I won't get a good job.'

'I expect you haven't thought of supper,' said Mum accusingly to Dad.

'I have. We've two pizzas in the freezer. The oven went on ages ago, so it's ready to cook, and I've got the stuff for a salad.'

'OK,' said Mum. 'But I've got to empty the washing machine from this morning as NOBODY has thought fit to do it.'

Mum brushed past me with the plastic laundry basket.

'Don't worry, love,' she said over her shoulder. 'Tests are nothing. You wait until you have real exams.'

So that's the sort of comfort and encouragement I get from my family.

The other problem about sharing my bedroom with my little brother is that there's no privacy. I think I should have my own bedroom, but we've only got the two.

After supper I nicked the radio in the kitchen while Mum was emptying the drier and tiptoed upstairs to my room. The coast was clear because Dad was bathing my brother. I twiddled the nobs until I found some thumping music from a station called Kiss FM. What a name! If Dad heard he would tease me mercilessly.

I stood in front of the mirror and stuck my bum out to one side, then to the other. It didn't look right somehow, so I tried a knee bend at the same time.

Then there was the problem of my arms.

I tried to remember *Top of the Pops.* I never watch it, except when my sixteen-year-old cousin Amy comes round. I wouldn't mind watching it, but Dad would only come in and make stupid remarks.

On *Top of the Pops* some of the dancers wave their arms over their heads, so I stuck my bum out, bent my knees up and down, and waved my arms.

Reflected in the mirror was a boy with big feet and boring mouse-coloured hair, blue eyes like Mum's and cheeks speckled with pink spots, wearing grey school trousers and a navy St David's sweatshirt, and jigging around like a lame kangaroo.

'Silly!'

Behind, in the mirror, stood a small boy, stark naked in the doorway.

'What did you say?' The music was so loud I wasn't sure I'd heard right.

'Silly . . . silly . . . silly,' chanted James, and he bounced into the room and started leaping about beside me, pretending to dance.

It was one of the most indecent sights I'd ever seen. There were bits of James bouncing up and down as he pranced around that shouldn't be seen in public.

'Come on, let's rave!' Dad swayed in through the door, clapping his hands, doing some tribal dance from his youth.

'James should have his pyjamas on,' I said. 'He's old

enough now to know he should wear something if he's going to leap around.'

'Since when so prim?' Dad laughed, still swaying to the music. 'He's only little. Oh . . . I forgot. You triple lock and padlock the bathroom now when you have your bath.'

'It's the only privacy I get in this house,' I yelled, stung by Dad's remark.

'I know, Matthew.' Dad stopped fooling around like one of those ancient rock stars. 'Turn the radio off, James, there's a good lad. We'll get that attic conversion worked out as soon as Mum and I have got used to this new job of hers.'

He'd been saying that for a year. Some hope, now Mum was so busy. These days they only had time to yell at each other at the weekends, between the supermarket shop, taking James to his swimming lesson, me to my karate, visiting Grandpa, cleaning the house, mowing the lawn, paying the bills and cooking the meals.

No . . . what really made me mad was not James's indecency or Dad behaving like a prehistoric pop star. It was their dancing. James jumped and jiggled, Dad clapped and swayed, but they did it in time, in rhythm with each other.

I looked all wrong. I didn't fit the music.

I was going to look a complete idiot at the disco.

So I knew I had to ask Josh about this dancing, because his brothers must have shown him a thing or two.

Four

At morning break the next day I caught up with Josh in the playground. Under his navy sweatshirt he was wearing a proper man's shirt with cuffs. They hung down over his hands so that I could see only his fingertips.

'Nice shirt,' I said.

Josh grunted.

'Have a spicy tandoori. They're not bad. Sort of mini crispy poppadoms.'

As Josh stuck his shirt sleeve in the crackling crisp bag, I saw he was wearing real cuff links. On one cuff link there was a large NO.

'Hey! Look at that,' I said. 'What's on the other one?'

Josh munched slowly and passed over his arm. The other cuff link had a large YES on it.

'Those are great! When you're watching telly and your mum tries to get you to hang up your school bag, you just hold up the NO.'

Josh didn't laugh. It's a shame that, because sometimes I think I'm very funny. Connor laughs at anything but not Josh. He just stared into the distance.

'Useful at discos, when the girls crowd in,' he muttered. 'You can take your pick . . . Hold up YES or NO.'

Visions of Zoe and Amanda charging me at the disco flashed through my mind. I wasn't sure I liked the picture. Amanda was a big girl and she'd tripped me up in the playground once, no trouble at all. A NO wouldn't stop her, and I wasn't sure she would take any notice of a YES either.

'Funny you should mention the disco, Josh,' I tried. 'Is . . . is it essential to dance at discos?'

I stuffed my mouth with a spicy tandoori.

'What else are you going to do at a disco?'

'But . . . I mean . . . this dancing. How do you learn it?'

Josh looked at me with an unfathomable flash of darkened glass and then looked away again. I felt a tug on my tandoori crisp packet and smacked my other hand down hard on Connor's grimy mitt.

'Keep off, Connor. You could have asked.'

I wasn't sharing my precious poppadoms with Connor as I knew he wouldn't teach me how to dance.

I stood there staring hopefully at Josh.

'How,' I repeated, 'do you learn?'

Josh shrugged. 'You don't. You just do it to the music.'

What a waste of a poppadom.

Connor stood there grinning as usual. 'Course,' he said, with his eyes glued to my tandoori packet, 'you've got no sense of rhythm, have you?'

I scratched my neck and pretended not to hear.

'Do you remember the time in Year Two,' he said, warming to the subject, 'when we had music lessons, before the school cut them to save money? You were playing the triangle and that music teacher . . . You remember . . . What was she called?'

'Hi!' I yelled at Adam and Harry.

They spotted us and headed our way.

'I remember,' went on Connor, like my grandpa's terrier gnawing away at Mum's sofa leg. 'She was called Miss Frankenstein or something, and she sent you out because you were making such a din, tinkling away on that triangle, all out of time.' Connor was doubled up now with giggles. 'She thought you were doing it on purpose. Don't you remember, Matthew? Your mum came storming into school, saying they were being mean to you, because the problem was you had NO EAR FOR MUSIC!'

'Going back into school?' I said casually to Adam, and I whisked my tandoori bag past Connor's nose and offered poppadoms to Adam, Harry and Josh.

I was ready to murder Connor. He was certainly never going to get a crisp from me again.

I couldn't shake him off, though. There he was, trailing us in, still talking.

'It's kind of interesting. Dad says there's an area of the brain, on the front lobe, that interprets rhythm, and that in people who can't hear a beat it's been damaged. I mean, did your mum ever drop you on your head on the kitchen floor?'

If Josh couldn't tell me how to dance, I seriously did not want to go to the disco. I'd look at Mum's *Family Medical Encyclopaedia*. Tummy pains . . . appendicitis, that sort of thing. I had to find some way of getting out of this nightmare. I might even run away until these tests and the disco were well and truly over.

You think things can't get any worse, but they always do. After break, Mrs Malpas, who teaches us general science, pounced the science test on us.

'But, Mrs Malpas,' shouted Adam, 'it's next week.'

'No, it isn't. It's today. You were warned last week by Mr Grinston.'

'No, we weren't.'

'Yes, you were. Now, Matthew, hand out this paper and get pens and pencils ready.'

'But it's unfair,' I said as I collected the pile of white paper off Mrs Malpas's desk.

Then I caught her eye and shut up.

Mrs Malpas is tiny, smaller than all of us, and round, like one of those squishy balls that babies play with. You'd think no one would take any notice of her, because there are some teachers like that, who shout and yell but everyone ignores. But Mrs Malpas is something else. I think she sends out invisible rays from her green eyes.

She stood there, silently waiting. The muttering faded away.

'Good,' she said, zapping us with her secret rays. 'Now, boys, I want you to enjoy this. It's all on what we've done this term and I've got some interesting questions for you.'

I walked round, handing out the paper.

Josh was sprawled across his desk. I winked at him, but I couldn't see if he winked back because of his shady glasses. I did see his knuckles, though, gripping his pencil, whiter than white.

Harry sat bolt upright, his black leather case, with lots of different compartments, open in front of him. All his pencils were newly sharpened – I expect the au pair does that – and I watched as he pulled out a shiny silver fountain pen, took off the cap and examined the gold nib.

Behind him, Adam jumped as I put the paper on his table. He'd been stuffing some screwed-up bits of printed page into the sleeve of his navy sweatshirt. What *could* he have been up to?

Connor gave me a big grin. General science is one of his favourite subjects, along with technology and maths. He had a ruler in front of him, a heap of big rubber bands, a compass and a roll of Sellotape. It looked as if he'd emptied his pockets out.

'What are the rubber bands for?' I whispered, curious.

'I tie the rubber bands together, attach the roll of Sellotape to the end and if I swing them round, the circular motion means the velocity—'

'That's enough chatting, Connor,' called Mrs Malpas.

If she hadn't interrupted, I might have learned something.

As I sat down I burped. It was a tandoori burp but it didn't taste spicy any more, more sour. I was sweating so much my shirt was clinging to my back.

'Turn over the test paper now!' called Mrs Malpas.

I couldn't believe it. The first question was: *Why do ships float?*

I knew that!

I unscrewed my rollerball and started writing: 'In ships there are lots of cabins and engine rooms. They are full of air. But air is not as dense as water so the ship floats.'

The test wasn't too bad. I couldn't do it all, but I could do most of it. I felt great afterwards.

'How did it go?' I asked Josh as we packed up to leave.

He shrugged. 'Boring.'

'Mmn,' I said. 'Boring.'

Then Connor came rushing up, grinning all over his freckled face.

'Did you get the ship question – Archimedes' Principle. Dad and I tried it out last week in the bath. We used a rubber ball and—'

Harry, carrying his black leather case, tried to push past. Connor grabbed his arm. 'Harry, did the CD do the job?'

We all stared with interest.

'Fine,' said Harry, who kept flicking his shiny hair out of his eyes. 'But I won't need science. My father is thinking of buying a biotechnology lab . . . Good investment for the future. We'll leave the science to the boffins.'

Connor stood there, his mouth gaping.

'Biotechnology . . . What sort?'

Harry ignored him. 'By the way, you lot. You can count Adam and me out of the disco. It'll be a pathetic party.'

'But the lights are going to be terrific . . .' began Connor, his eyes wide with dismay.

'When you've seen the lights in New York . . .' Harry gave a laugh. 'I mean, a first-year disco, in the school gym . . .'

Adam yawned noisily.

'But Adam's never been to New York,' said Connor angrily.

'We're not going,' said Adam, jutting his chin up close to Connor. 'It's for wimps who've got nothing better to do than fiddle around with coloured bulbs and electric wires.'

'Yeah,' said Josh.

So I knew Josh wouldn't be going either.

I looked at Connor and I could see he was hurt. I felt

bad letting him down, as he'd been my best mate at primary school. But times change. And I couldn't dance.

'School gym?' and I tried a Josh chuckle, but it came out squeaky again. 'I wouldn't be seen dead there.'

I was walking on air. I'd survived the first test and got out of the disco. I wouldn't have to make a fool of myself in front Zoe and Amanda.

Or so I thought. But events never seem to work out the way you want.

Five

On the bus going home, we Year Sevens sit at the front. Nobody tells us to, but the older boys get mad if we take the best seats at the back.

I reckon there were about twenty of us from the three classes of the first year and we talked of nothing but the disco.

'It's going to be useless,' I said to Luke Riley, who used to be a mate of mine in primary school although he's now in one of the parallel classes.

'Why?' said Luke.

He's not too bright Luke, and he likes everything spelled out nice and clear.

'It's old Grinston trying to impress the new head. He wants to prove he's not past it, because he's too old to be a year head.'

'Are you going, Josh?' Luke tried.

'Nah . . . It won't be a proper disco,' muttered Josh, and he stared out of the window as if it was all a chronic bore.

'I've never been to a disco,' went on Luke. 'I thought I'd give it a try.'

Adam, who hadn't got a lift home in Harry's Explorer, as Harry had rushed off after the science test, stuck his bristly head round the side of the seat in front to listen.

'There'll be girls there,' Luke tried again.

There was a snort from Adam. 'What girls? You mean Amanda, Zoe, Ellen and Katrina, Samantha, Jo, Melanie . . . that lot! Call them girls!'

I was puzzled. I thought they were girls.

'They're just stupid, giggly schoolkids,' said Adam nastily. 'We remember that lot. I can't be bothered with them.'

Adam had been bothered with them all right at primary school. The girls used to refuse to sit on the same table as him, because they said he pinched them and he spoilt their drawings.

I nodded but I couldn't help feeling a bit guilty. I quite liked Amanda, even if she did trip me up in the playground and she was always breaking things. And Zoe's mum had been best friends with my mum when we were little, so we used to play at each other's house.

Connor sat opposite me across the gangway. He didn't say a word, but he kept on at his little notebook with his drawings of the gym and diagrams of the different lighting systems.

'If you're all not going, then I'm not going,' decided Luke finally.

'I'm going to see the new James Bond instead the Friday term ends,' said Sam.

'Got plenty of real girls in that,' smirked Kevin.

'I'll come too,' said Luke's mate, Shiva. 'What about you, Connor? The baddy's got this armoured bulldozer that'll knock down houses, go over a mountain of rubble, and it's amphibious too, so it can attack yachts.'

'No,' Connor muttered.

'No!' said Adam scornfully. 'You don't mean you're going to go to that pathetic disco?'

'I am,' said Connor. 'I promised I'd work on the lights.'

It was Mum's turn to finish early. When I got home she was slumped at the kitchen table, having a mug of tea with my cousin Amy. James was watching children's telly in the living room, so I tried to grab my chance and tiptoe upstairs to the bedroom.

'My mum is the strictest mum I know . . .' Amy's usual moan drifted up the stairs. 'She won't let me buy these shoes, even though it's my money. She says she's responsible for me until I'm eighteen and until then I'm to do what she thinks best.'

'Amy, your mum told me about the shoes. She says they're lethal, with tall, spiky heels. They'll ruin your feet and you'll get bunions. And anyway, heels that high are bad for your back.'

'But I was only going to wear them on Saturday nights. Can you say something to her? She's your sister.'

'Well . . . if it's only Saturday nights . . . I'll talk to her about it.'

'I wish you were my mum.'

Amy's mother, Aunty Eileen, is really nice. She doesn't get into the states my mum does and you don't have endless ready-made meals at their house. Aunty Eileen cooks delicious stuff like chicken casseroles with dumplings, followed by apple crumble and ice cream.

Whenever Amy has a row with her mum, and she seems to have more and more of them, she rushes round to our house, saying she'd rather have our mum. It means even less attention for me, and she eats all the biscuits, which is bad news, since Dad and Mum only go shopping once a week now, on Saturdays.

The top step creaked under my foot.

'Hey, gorgeous!' Amy's silly voice rang up the stairs. 'I can hear you!'

'You might come and say hello, Matthew, as I'm home early,' called Mum. 'The kettle is still hot. Get a tea bag out and make yourself a mug of tea,' she said as I gave up and joined them in the kitchen.

I threw my wet tea bag on top of the grot bursting out of the rubbish bin.

'I've heard all about the disco,' grinned Amy. She's sixteen, with lips painted a gooey strawberry red. 'Big

34

boy now. First disco.' And she reached over and ruffled my hair.

I hate that.

Amy's four years older than me, and when I was little she used to take me out in my pushchair and push me up and down the road in front of our house with some of her girlfriends. I was just a big doll for her to dress up and coo over. Even then I was wised up enough to know how to exploit it.

I played the baby boy role for quite a few years, and it certainly paid off in sweets. Now I find her sickening, with her I'm-so-much-more-grown-up-than-you ways.

'So when's the big party?'

'Two weeks' time.'

'And what are we wearing for it? Something stunning and trendy. You can come with me and the girls on Saturday to the market, if you like. We'll soon fix you up.'

'I'm not going.'

Mum put her mug down on the table. She didn't look so tired tonight. She had done her hair in a plait down her back, and that takes time, and her blue eyes didn't have that glassy stare.

'Not going, Matthew? Of course you'll go.'

'It's going to be pathetic. Mr Grinston is trying to impress the new head and buy popularity. It's in the gym, which is terrible and pongs of stinky trainers, and they're just a silly lot of giggly girls coming from St Anne's.'

Mum laughed.

'Matthew, it'll be a lot of work for Mr Grinston. You should be seeing how you can help to make it a good party and giving him some support.'

'I don't want to go. I'll hate it, I know.'

'But you don't know until you try.'

They were both smiling at me, as if I was doing comedy or something.

'Go on, Matty,' said Amy in her silly voice. 'Give it a whirl. Me and the girls will get you up something gorgeous.'

'No, I'm not going, so shut up both of you.'

'Matthew!' said Mum. 'I won't have you talking like that. You must be hungry . . . Oh dear, was that the last biscuit, Amy? Well . . . it won't be long now until supper.'

When Dad mooched in for supper, his shoulders sagged and he had his robot switched on.

'He says he's not going to the disco,' started Mum, 'and I said we'd see about that . . .'

'Not going to the disco,' Dad nodded, as he shovelled peas into his mouth.

'He should support the school, and particularly Mr Grinston.'

'Support the school . . .' Dad echoed.

'I did my science test today, Dad.'

I was anxious to divert the conversation, because after Dad's had a bit to eat he comes to life and the robot switches off.

'How did it go?'

'OK, but I've got loads more tests.'

'What did I tell you? Fine school like St David's, you've nothing to worry . . . Just look at that rubbish bucket! What was it about modern marriages?'

Mum sat up straight, very still.

'The bed was unmade when I got in from work.' Her blue eyes were flashing dangerously. 'Who's meant to make it when I go early?'

'I had to get James to school and we couldn't find his reading book,' said Dad crossly.

I slipped out of the kitchen and escaped upstairs. The voices bounced back and forth below like barbed ping-pong balls.

I wished they'd stop, but at least they'd forgotten the disco.

At school the next day there we all were, lounging over the tiers in the school hall, thinking, Poor old Grinston when he hears most of us are giving the disco a miss.

He droned on about a test in this and a test in that, and getting a good night's sleep and how to revise thoroughly and eat a good breakfast. It was meant to be encouraging, but it only made me more nervous.

'Enough of that,' he said at last, as he took his specs off and stared up at us. He gave a little cough. 'I'm afraid, boys, that I have some very disappointing news.'

No . . . We couldn't all have failed the science test.

The rows of boys were unusually silent, watching Mr

Grinston shift from one foot to another, his mouth twitching as he attempted to smile.

'The disco . . . the Christmas disco.'

I looked at Josh with a knowing smile. Behind us Adam groaned, while Harry drummed with his knuckles on his knees. Here and there I glimpsed the odd smirk and heard a bored sigh.

'I'm afraid we may have to cancel it.'

Fantastic! That solved everything. I didn't even have to feel guilty.

'Why, sir?' Connor piped up on the other side of me.

I leaned towards Josh. I didn't want any of the year thinking I had anything to do with Connor.

'I'm afraid,' said Mr Grinston slowly, 'that the uptake on the tickets at St Anne's has been very poor indeed. In fact we haven't had a single request for a ticket.'

Six

As we walked out of the hall none of us knew where to look. Nobody mucked around as usual and the silence was creepy.

I mean, not wanting to make a fool of myself at the disco was one thing, but to be rejected by every girl at St Anne's before they'd even seen me dance was another. I was surprised how disappointed I was at the thought of not seeing Amanda, because I knew Mum would have made me go to the disco in the end. And I had a suspicion from the silence the others were disappointed too. But none of us could say anything, because we'd all said we wouldn't be seen dead at the disco anyway.

'Dad and I had these great plans for the lights. I was going to show Mr Grinston today,' Connor said, not seeming to notice the silent gloom in the passage as we tramped along. 'Perhaps I can use some of the ideas for an electronics project. Yeah, that would be great. I could do a project on designing disco lighting.'

'Shut up, Connor,' said Adam, aiming a kick at Connor's ankle. 'Who's interested in boring electronics and stupid projects?'

'Ow!' yelled Connor. 'What did you do that for?'

Adam drew back his foot as if a second kick was going to follow the first. I hooked my leg in quickly and caught his foot as it came forward. He went flying. Amanda would've been proud of me.

Amanda. I'd never see her now.

Harry moved to help Adam up, but, as he bent over, his smart black leather case caught Luke across his face. For a second Luke didn't understand what had hit him. He put his hand up to his face and then stared at the drop of blood on his palm.

I moved back. This was going to be dangerous.

It takes a bit to get Luke angry, because he doesn't understand things too quickly, but when he gets angry . . . watch out!

In the end it wasn't clear who was fighting whom. I saw Luke's arm flying, Harry plunging dramatically to the floor, Connor neatly dodging out of the way, Adam sidling carefully round the group and aiming some well-placed kicks. Josh stashed his smart specs on the windowsill, but I'm not sure he could see too much as he was punching air most of the time. Then Kevin appeared out of nowhere and dived in, and I thought, Why not? and tried out a few karate moves.

(I must remember to have a word with my karate instructor, because the moves didn't work. None of the others took up the positions I was waiting for.)

'What *is* going on here?'

The shrill voice broke my concentration as I was trying to get Connor to take up a fighting position so that I could get a back-hold on him.

It was Mrs Malpas. Somehow her green hypnotic rays shot through the heaving tangle of boys and I let go of Connor.

'We take a serious view of any fighting on school premises,' she said as her tiny, plump hands tugged us apart. 'This is utterly disgraceful. Harry, is that your smart case with your books being trampled on the floor? Pick it up and put it away, and Luke, get up off the floor this minute.'

Luke groaned as he stood up, clutching his cheek.

'Let me see,' demanded Mrs Malpas. 'You can go to the school nurse if . . . But that's just a scratch.'

'It was bleeding,' said Luke sullenly.

'It's stopped bleeding. Now, I'm not going to ask what this was about, or whose fault it was, but if I catch you fighting again it's straight to the head. You'd better hurry or you'll be late for your next class.'

We all raced off, relieved to have escaped a trip to the head, and Mrs Malpas wasn't as cross as she could have been. I reckon she knew we were letting off steam.

41

Not a single ticket . . . Not one girl wanted to come to the disco!

It was Josh who came up with the explanation. At lunch I bought a packet of smoked ham niblets in the canteen. There were stacks of them on the counter and nothing else resembling a decent crisp. They tasted off. Niblets should be cheese and crisps should be smoked ham – anyone who knows anything about crisps would agree with that.

I held them out to Josh and Connor. 'You can have them, they're disgusting.'

'Generous, I'm sure,' said Josh, ignoring the proffered bag.

'Don't mind if I do,' said Connor, taking a handful. 'Makes a change from ready-salted.'

Connor crunched a niblet and smiled. 'Delicious!'

Connor has a nice face when he smiles, with browny-green eyes that crinkle at the corner and smudgy freckles sprinkled over his cheeks even in winter. If he didn't have that ridiculous haircut, he'd have been in with a chance. As his hair is, I wasn't surprised no girl from St Anne's wanted . . . No, the rejection was too big. I couldn't bear to admit it to myself.

'Josh, you know about discos. Why do you think the girls don't want to come?'

'Don't like us,' suggested Connor cheerfully.

Josh looked at Connor as if he was an annoying fly that needed swatting.

'Could be lots of things,' he said perceptively.

'Like what?'

'The venue could be wrong.'

'The venue?' I asked.

'The gym . . . it's not good. Everyone knows you gotta have a good venue.'

I thought about the gym. It was disgustingly smelly, but surely the St Anne's girls couldn't know about that if they had never been in it before.

'And there's the publicity. You need posters and flyers.'

'Mr Grinston said he'd put a notice up on the main board at St Anne's. The girls are supposed to walk past it every day on their way into assembly. They *must* have seen it.'

'Do you look at the school board every day?' said Harry as he put down his tray, laden with cans of cola, Mars bars and KitKats. 'I've got better things to do.'

Adam followed close behind. Silently, Harry threw him a Mars bar.

'What's this about the school notice board?' Adam sniggered as he tore off the wrapping. 'Bet you can't guess who changed the teams round for the Saturday under-fourteens so that stupid Luke believed he'd been selected as captain.'

I sort of smiled and knew I was a coward. It was a mean trick to play on Luke, but I don't like to get on the wrong side of Adam.

'Publicity,' murmured Josh. 'You need good publicity for an event. Publicity . . . publicity . . .'

'Disc got stuck?' said Adam, his mouth crammed with gooey toffee and chocolate.

We all stared at Josh as he banged his forehead with his fist. 'Got it!'

We jumped. Josh never usually shouts.

'A billboard, a hoarding beside a road . . . That's what we need. Something they can't possibly miss.'

'And if they know about the disco, do you think they'll come?' I said.

Josh nodded wisely. 'Good publicity always works,' he explained.

And we all began to feel quite cheerful again, because although none of us would admit it, I think we would all have gone along in a gang to the disco, pretending we didn't want to be there.

Of course the girls had missed Mr Grinston's notice. They needed to see a huge hoarding. Their not coming was nothing to do with us, just bad publicity.

And that was why, after school, Harry sent the Jeep with the au pair home empty, saying he had to stay late, and Josh, me, Harry and Adam followed Connor down Stormont Road, to where all the stinking-rich houses are.

There, outside number 42, The Pines, was a sign saying:

House Refurbishment by Ogden Building Services.
Architect: Leo Sidebotham, BA (Arch) RIBA

And in the road beneath the sign there was this great yellow skip crammed full of useful building material – old wooden boards, curtain poles, discarded kitchen cupboards – just waiting for us to pick over.

seven

It was dark when we got back to my house, which was a relief as we had a mountain of stuff with us. There'd been a bit of a dispute as to where it would be best to build the hoarding.

Harry has the biggest garden, but he had spent every second minute dodging down inside the skip when anyone had walked past The Pines. It turned out that his house was only round the corner and he was afraid some of the neighbours might recognise him.

'We're not doing anything illegal,' said Josh. 'This stuff is building rubbish. The skip men will only go and drop it in some great rubbish tip.'

'Sort of recycling,' I suggested, as I wrestled a long wooden curtain pole out from under dusty bags of old plaster.

'Our au pair only recycles in special coloured boxes,' said Harry, 'and the council comes to collect them.'

'But you've plenty of room on your front lawn,' protested Josh.

'Front lawn!' Harry's voice rose in horror.

I could see his point. Harry's front lawn looks as if it has been cut by an army of gardeners with nail scissors.

'Our flat is on the second floor,' said Connor, 'and we've only got a tiny corner of the cellar for storage. We keep our suitcases there.'

Nobody mentioned Adam's house. Things have a nasty habit of disappearing at his place. Even the police go looking for lost stuff there and we didn't want them accusing us of having nicked a billboard.

'We'll have to go to Matthew's, then,' said Josh. 'We can dump everything in your back garden. We'll come round and make it this weekend.'

'For the disco?' queried Mum, staring out of the kitchen window at the mound on the back lawn.

It was Saturday morning. What with the mad panic of rushing off to work early, getting James to school and coming home in the dark, neither she nor Dad had noticed our growing pile of supplies.

'But that's a load of old rubbish . . . What do you want with those broken kitchen units, and there's a door, and a three-legged chair on top. It's junk. It'll ruin the lawn.'

'Just until the disco, Mum . . . please.'

'But you said you weren't going to the disco.'

'Did I?'

I'd forgotten. My stomach turned over, churning my Coco Krispies so badly that I suddenly didn't fancy the toast that popped out of the toaster.

I'd have to dance. Make a fool of myself.

With not a single ticket sold to a St Anne's girl, it had seemed the most important thing in the world to save the respect of Year Seven. We'd all look really stupid if it got out that the girls hadn't wanted to come to our disco. People might start thinking there was something wrong with us, even though I was sure we didn't look much different from any other boys our age. Or could it be there *was* something odd about us?

We were doing the right thing. We had to get the girls from St Anne's there, if only to prove we were OK.

Perhaps I could help Connor with the lighting. Then I'd be so busy I wouldn't have time to dance.

'We're going to make a billboard, to advertise the disco. Josh is working on the plan.'

'Sounds a great idea,' said Dad, carefully laying rashers of bacon in the grill pan. 'All the lads together, eh?'

'But it's such a mess out there,' said Mum doubtfully.

'We'll clear up, Mum, promise. And it's for school.'

'I can't see why you're not making it at school, then.'

'It's a surprise for Mr Grinston,' I said truthfully. 'We're helping out, joining in, like you said I should.'

'Well . . . OK,' said Mum. 'Look after the house while Dad and I go to the supermarket.'

Five minutes after Mum and Dad had left for the supermarket, Harry's au pair dropped him off in the Jeep.

'Did you bring some tools?'

'No luck,' said Harry. 'My father says he doesn't have any. The handyman brings his own.'

'What are you going to do, then?' I said unkindly.

Harry looked lost for a moment and then flashed his toothy white smile. 'I'll hold the wood steady for you to saw.'

I'd raided the shed and found a hammer, a rusty saw and some long nails. Then Adam clattered in with a walking armoury. There were saws, chisels and tools I'd never even seen before.

'What's this long wire with a hook on the end for?'

'Helps you get in a car when you've lost your keys.' Adam grinned.

Connor ran up in torn trousers and a sweater with an elbow sticking out of the sleeve.

'Dressed for the disco, then, Connor?' said Adam, and we all chuckled. But Connor doesn't even notice remarks like that.

Then Josh slunk in, wearing a full-length black coat. He looked fantastic, like Count Dracula. His hands were completely amputated by the long sleeves and it was muddy at the back where the coat trailed on the ground. Out of a deep pocket he pulled a tiny hammer and a handful of small screwdrivers.

'Where'd you get those?' I asked.

'My brother keeps them by his sound system. Have to take them back.'

If it had been Connor, I would have made some joke about tiny tools for leprechauns, but Josh is too . . . dignified for jokes like that.

'Got the plan, then?' I asked.

Josh waited while we all watched, then he pushed back the sleeves of his coat and fished in his pocket. 'Here it is,' he announced, unfolding a sheet of paper.

We stared. It was a good picture all right, but then Josh is good at art. It was a giant hoarding with brilliant red lettering. Underneath cars as small as beetles were driving past, and a little crowd of girls the size of ants was staring up at it.

Adam sneered, 'How do you think we're going to make that?'

'It's almost as big as the Empire State Building,' joked Harry.

Josh looked pained but didn't seem to have an answer.

I was disappointed. I had thought Josh was on to something great.

Connor took the piece of paper and sucked his tongue loudly. 'We can scale it down, sort of make a miniature version. We'll take the old door, cut it down to a squarer shape, attach the long curtain poles to the

50

back to support the weight and cut the feet off the kitchen chair to support the bottom.'

You have to give it to Connor, he knows his stuff. Josh sniffed and nodded as if that was what he had meant all along.

It was freezing out in the garden, but at least it wasn't raining. We kept blowing on our hands as Connor showed us how to saw wood, hammer in nails straight and screw on hinges.

Harry made us tea and coffee.

'How many spoonfuls of coffee in a mug?' he called.

I reckon he'd never made a cup of coffee before. He looked quite pleased with himself when he brought it all over on a tray and he'd even dug out red paper napkins from somewhere.

We stopped for a break, warming our hands round the mugs. This was great. We had sawn up wood, broken up old kitchen doors and bits of pole, there was sawdust everywhere ... I hadn't had such a good time since Connor and I used to work on our Lego projects.

'Oh, my God!' Mum staggered past, bulging plastic bags in both hands. 'What's all this mess?'

We all looked up in surprise. Mess? We nearly had the billboard finished.

Dad staggered in after her.

'Just look at that, Simon. Ruining the lawn, and ... yes ... the red paper napkins trampled in the mud, the ones I bought last week for Christmas.'

'We'll get some more.'

'It's your fault. You encouraged him, with that "great idea" and "all lads together."'

'That's not correct, Sue. I distinctly heard you say "OK" to Matthew.'

'You take every little word I say literally,' yelled Mum.

'Well, what is it supposed to mean if it doesn't mean what it should mean?'

They were at it again. This was getting dangerous.

'Mrs Evans, may I carry your shopping in for you?' Harry flashed his most nauseating toothy smile.

'Uh . . . yes, Harry, that would be a great help.'

'You must be tired after such a big shop.'

'I am, Harry, I'm exhausted.'

We stared in astonishment. Harry is such a smoothy. Where does he learn manners like that? I guess it's the only thing his parents care about, as they're always having all these parties and dinners. I don't know when they get the time to talk to Harry, because the house is full of guests most of the time or they're away on trips.

Manners . . . We didn't know what those were in our house. Mum and Dad were always yelling at each other so much, they didn't have time to teach us.

Once the last bag of shopping was in, we kept on working without any more comments from Mum. Dad even brought out some cheese sandwiches and a couple of packets of biscuits. There went next week's biscuits, but at least they wouldn't be in Amy's greedy stomach.

From his other coat pocket Josh fished out two battered spray cans.

'Touch-up paint,' he explained. 'From my brothers' cars.'

We looked at Adam. We'd seen him spraying graffiti on the wall behind the music room. In fact several other people had seen him too and it had taken him quite a few breaks to clean the wall with the caretaker.

'Sure, I'll do it,' he said.

Josh told him what to write and he was brilliant.

It looked like this:

DISCO!
The most sensational, wildest, coolest,
mega-disco of the year!
Stunning lights
St David's Year Seven calling St Anne's Year Seven
Friday, 16 December, 7 p.m. till late
Tickets from Mr Grinston, St David's,
or on the door

Josh led the way out of our backyard, with Connor and me carrying the front and Harry carrying the back.

'I'll stay and clear up the tools,' said Adam.

'No,' said Connor suddenly, dropping down his side. 'If you so much as touch a tool that isn't yours . . .'

'Help Harry carry at the back,' I said quickly.

Josh walked in front, flashing the torch Connor had thought to bring like a police car alarm light, so that we wouldn't get mown down by the cars going shopping or to Saturday football matches.

Eight

To get to St Anne's you walk along the main road and then turn off left down a side road for about 500 metres, past the golf course until you reach the school gates. Before and after school there are streams of cars packed with girls. The school bus arrives that way too, because Josh and I have watched it before.

Getting the board up wasn't that easy. The curtain poles kept slipping sideways and when they were upright they tilted the board too far forwards over the kitchen chair legs. Eventually Josh, Adam, Harry and I held a leg each while Connor shortened the back legs by pushing them deep in the ground.

We stood back and surveyed the billboard. It looked all right. A fraction of the size of Josh's original, but it did the trick.

We had a pretend karate fight then and there, until a golfer in a tartan cap called over the fence, 'Cut that out, boys.'

I wonder when it is you get so old that you can't tell the difference between pretend and real any more.

Adam made a rude noise and the golfer waved his club at us, and we set off laughing loudly back to the main road home.

'Good, you're back,' said Mum as I walked in to the kitchen. 'The mess on the back lawn is dreadful. What are you going to do about it?'

'We did clear up.'

'Call that clearing up! You're going to have to go out there with black rubbish bags and clear the whole lot up again.'

'Now?' I groaned.

'Tomorrow, Sunday. You're coming shopping with me now, down the market.'

I hate shopping. Usually I protest loudly, but I didn't dare with Mum being so cross about the lawn. Not that I could see anything wrong with it – there were just a few old poles, chair seats, sawdust and a kitchen cupboard door that we hadn't used.

Mum's face was grim as we drove into town.

'I don't know why I'm so good to you, what with all the pressures on my time these days.'

Since when has shopping been good news? I thought.

The light was fading as we parked in a side street. The market was lit up with coloured bulbs round the stalls. Most were decorated with glittery tinsel and plastic holly, and loudspeakers everywhere were belting out carols and 'Rudolph the Red-nosed Reindeer'. I tripped over a stack of Christmas trees leaning against a fruit and veg stall.

'Steady, son,' said the stallkeeper lady, wagging a bright red nail at me. 'You should go easy on the drinking now.'

Mum laughed.

She stopped in front of a stall covered with hundreds of shirts. Even more hung like flags from the roof. There were football shirts, shirts with sparkly psychedelic patterns, hippie tie-dyed shirts and shirts in brilliant stripes.

'Looking for yourself, lady?' said the man at the back, stuffing twenty-pound notes into a leather pouch strapped round his fat waist.

He reached out and pulled down from an overhead hanger a pale blue T-shirt with sparkly dark blue bits which spelt out *BEAUTIFUL! That's me.*

'Matches your eyes, love,' said the man. 'Makes them even more beautiful.'

Mum giggled.

I didn't like the man, smirking at Mum in his black leather jacket. Dad never talks like that, so I was surprised at Mum giggling.

'No. It's for my son here. He's going to his first disco. Now, what's the thing to wear these days?'

I could have crawled under the stall.

That's right: tell the world I've never been to a disco. Tell them I can't dance while you're about it.

An old lady was picking over some cut-price shirts in a bin.

'A disco? That'll be nice, love,' she said. 'How about taking me? I like a bit of dancing myself, but my old man's past it.'

I smiled weakly. Typical – a joke for the grown-ups to embarrass me.

'Right, son,' said the grinning stallholder, waving a cigarette in brown-stained fingers. 'Disco, eh? There'll be some nice girls you'll want to impress.' He gave me a wink. 'I know just the shirt for the job.'

He pulled out a red T-shirt with orange bands. It hurt my eyes to look at it. If I appeared in that, no one could fail to notice my lousy dancing.

'Cheerful,' said Mum. 'What do you think, Matthew?'

I was speechless with horror.

'It's loud . . . but fun, don't you think?'

'No, Mum,' I managed. 'No. I AM NOT WEARING THAT.'

'Keep your hair on, son,' said the man in the black jacket. 'That's no way to talk to your mum when she's buying you a present.'

'I know, Matthew,' said Mum. 'You have a good browse and I'll nip and get some oranges from the fruit and veg stall.'

I kept turning over the T-shirts. The stallholder

dropped his silly patter and eyed me coldly as he dragged on his cigarette.

'Fold them up, son, when you've looked. I'm not having my stall turned into a trash heap by some pimply boy who doesn't know what he wants.'

I held up a blue one, but it was miles too long. I needed something inconspicuous.

'Have you got a brown shirt?'

'What's that, son? A brown shirt? Who'd wear a brown T-shirt to a disco?'

What could I wear? It was panic stations all round. I didn't know what you wore for a disco and I didn't want to look a fool.

Mum was coming back. The stallholder saw her and leaned over to me.

'Look, I'll let you into a secret, son. This mustard-yellow one here, which has got a bit of brown edging which you said you wanted, it's your colour. Suits you. Not too loud, a bit of class. Says "This lad knows what he's about."'

He held it up against me.

'See,' he said to Mum as she reached the stall, 'he's made an excellent choice. Real taste, your boy.'

'Do you think so?' said Mum, smiling happily. 'I'm a bit out of touch myself.'

'Doesn't he look handsome?'

'Handsome?' said Mum in surprise.

I cringed, but then I thought, Perhaps he means it.

★

At home I put the shirt on while James was having tea downstairs. I'd never worn anything that colour before. Mustard yellow, the man called it. It had a V neck and long sleeves that were a bit too short.

I switched on the radio, Kiss FM again, and practised my dancing.

Perhaps it looked better in the mustard shirt. Maybe I was learning how to do the knee-bobbing stuff.

'Turn that din off!' yelled Dad, bursting into my room.

'You didn't knock,' I said accusingly.

'You wouldn't have heard even if I had with that rubbish on. What is it?'

'Kiss FM.'

'Kiss FM!' guffawed Dad. 'That's a good one! Kiss, did you say?' He unplugged the radio. 'Gets on my nerves, that din thumping away. That's enough of Kiss for today,' and he smacked a noisy kiss in my direction as he left.

I was mad but I didn't dare protest. He might have come back to watch my dancing and I didn't want any more rude gestures from him. At least he hadn't noticed my new shirt. I wasn't sure whether that was a good sign or not.

Nine

Sunday I had to clear up the back lawn. Mum was right. There were more supplies around than I remembered. There was no way I was going to stuff doors from kitchen units into flimsy black plastic bags, let alone put them out for the rubbish men.

'Need a hand, Matthew?'

'Dad, what am I going to do with this lot? Mum said I'm not getting any lunch until the lawn is clear.'

That was a cruel threat. The one meal worth eating these days in our house is Sunday lunch. Mum and Dad cook it together, to make us 'feel like a proper family'. Today was roast lamb. I smelled it when Dad opened the door and came out.

Dad stood looking at the dismantled kitchen units, chair legs and curtain poles we hadn't got round to using. 'Load of old junk. Did you get your board made?'

'It's brilliant, Dad. We've got it up already.'

'I know what we'll do,' said Dad. 'Let's get the saw out, cut this lot up into manageable pieces and stack them against the back wall of the shed.'

'But Mum will only call it rubbish.'

'Next summer we'll build a brick barbecue and we'll use the wood as fuel.'

'OK,' I said doubtfully, as Dad set to sawing.

I held the wood steady and stacked the pieces behind the back of the shed.

'Dad, aren't you going to do the loft extension for my bedroom first?'

'We can build them both. You've got to think big in life, Matthew.'

It was hard work sawing and stacking the wood.

The kitchen window banged open.

'Do I have to call you four times for lunch,' Mum shouted, 'or do you like burnt lamb?'

It was tender lamb with mint jelly and peas and roast potatoes and gravy . . . the best.

I hoped Dad was right about thinking big, because, on balance, I'd rather have a loft bedroom of my own than a barbecue.

Monday and Tuesday weren't bad. Monday we had the maths test and, as I think I've modestly told you, I'm good at maths.

After school Josh and I headed out of the gates to Mr Patel's shop. I was rich, as Mum had given me my pocket money at the weekend. I'd nipped in with Josh before Connor caught up with us. Mr Patel only allows two schoolchildren in at a time, so Connor wouldn't be able to muscle in on us.

'Crisps for you two?'

He knows his customers, does Mr Patel.

'Cracked pepper and vinegar,' I said.

'I'll try that new garlic sausage flavour in the striped bag,' said Josh.

'So how are the exams going?' said Mr Patel as he took our money.

'Awful,' said Josh. 'I've just failed the maths. I couldn't do any of it.'

'Did you work hard? Were you studious?' said Mr Patel.

'Urgh ... sort of ... Not really. I hate maths. Nobody is going to make me do work I don't like.'

'When my little Vijay is at St David's I will make sure he works hard.' Mr Patel had begun wagging a long brown finger at Josh. 'That way he will do well in his exams, go to college, be a doctor or engineer, have a nice family with a big house and car, and not have to get up like me at five o'clock in the morning to take in the morning papers and organise the paper rounds.'

Parents are all the same. Mr Patel goes on like my mum: work hard, exams, college, good jobs ...

Mr Patel is a nice man, and he knows a lot about

63

crisps, but he'd made me worried all over again. If he goes on like this, I shall take my custom to the news-agent five minutes further down the road, except I know I'm too lazy to change now.

'Did the maths go that badly?' I said to Josh as I tried one of his garlic sausage crisps.

Josh shrugged his shoulders.

'Well . . . do you want to go to college, and all that?' I asked. 'I mean, what do you want to be when you grow up?'

'Bodyguard.'

'Bodyguard?'

'Yup.'

'Why do you want to be a bodyguard?'

'Great shades, and you have a smart suit and you get to travel all over the place, protecting famous pop stars.'

I munched, thinking.

I'd never have thought of a job like that. That's what comes of having sophisticated older brothers. But Josh isn't the best fighter. He's hopeless at karate, unless he has his glasses on, which he isn't allowed to do in our classes. Now Adam *would* make a good bodyguard, because he's quick and wiry and tough.

A hand fell on my back.

'What a pong! What have you two been eating?'

Connor pinched his nose shut with his fingers, so that he sounded as if he had a bad cold.

'Garlic sausage crisps,' said Josh. 'Try one, they're interesting.'

'Not on your life. I'm sticking to my plain.'

'Haven't you got through that special buy from Ready Save yet?' I asked unkindly.

'No. Mum thought they were such a bargain she bought a second lot,' Connor said, grinning and quite missing my sarcasm. You could stick pins into Connor, and he wouldn't notice, because there's always so much else going on in his mind.

'Well, that's maths over,' he said. 'It didn't go too badly.'

'Connor,' I asked, 'have you thought about what you're going to do when you leave school?'

'I'm going to college to study electrical engineering, so maths will come in handy. What about you?'

'I'm going to . . . sort of . . .'

I hadn't a clue.

Harry stepped out of Mr Patel's carrying four cans of cola, a packet of chocolate digestives and two Nuttee ice creams on sticks. They're the ones coated in nuts and chocolate with toffee ice cream inside. He passed a Nuttee on to Adam, who was practically salivating behind him.

'Want some chocolate biscuits?' said Harry. 'The au pair's late. She's unreliable, this one.'

We grabbed the packet of biscuits and split it open.

'Hold on,' laughed Harry.

He thought we were having a friendly tussle, but I knew we were just greedy and recognised a free biscuit when we saw one.

'I've only got four cans of cola,' said Harry. 'Sorry, Connor. I only saw Josh and Matthew go ahead of us into Mr Patel's.'

'That's OK,' said Connor. 'I don't want any.'

That set me thinking. Connor never seemed to be in Mr Patel's any more.

'I can't drink all this,' I said after a couple of swigs. 'Connor, do you want to finish it?'

'OK,' said Connor, and he downed the lot.

So he did want a cola after all.

'What was that about college you were talking about when Adam and I came out of Mr Patel's?' said Harry, licking the last drips of ice cream off his hands.

'When you leave school,' I said, 'what will you do?'

'I might go to college,' said Harry. 'But then, exams are never going to be very important for me. My father has quite a few businesses going, and I expect I'll take over one or two of them. And I'll do a spot of travelling . . . round the world.'

'What about you, Adam?' I asked, feeling more desperate. Everyone seemed to know but me. Was I destined to be one of life's losers?

'I'll go where the money is.' He laughed. 'Get my hands on some dosh.'

Harry had better watch out.

'Why so gloomy, Matthew?' laughed Harry, throwing back his shiny mane of hair. 'You can always marry a rich girl.'

'A rich girl? Where do you find a rich girl?'

I'd have been happy enough with an ordinary girl . . . like Amanda. That creep at the stall had said I was handsome in the yellow shirt, and my dancing was definitely improving. Maybe Amanda would recognise me at the disco. 'Hi, it's Matthew!' she'd say, and I'd say something cool like, 'Long time, no see,' and we'd dance.

'That reminds me,' said Harry suddenly. 'I saw Mr Grinston on the way out of school and he says he's still not had a single request from St Anne's for a ticket.'

We stared at each other.

So it hadn't worked. I was surprised how disappointed I was, but then I felt relieved that I wouldn't have to make a fool of myself with the dancing.

'It doesn't surprise me,' said Harry. 'I thought that billboard was rather an amateur attempt.'

'Pathetic,' agreed Adam.

'Mmn,' said Josh, as if the idea had been nothing to do with him.

'My father knows a good designer,' began Harry.

'No time!' I said cheerfully.

Only Connor was silent, staring down intently at his battered trainers. 'Hold on,' he started. 'I know . . . It's the light . . . Yes, the dim light. December is so dark in the morning and again in the afternoon, you don't notice a thing. We've got to catch their attention.'

'Going to put on an electricity supply for some lights, are we?' sniggered Adam.

'No, but I've got an idea. Will someone come along to my gran's house with me before school tomorrow?'

The silence was deafening. Harry, Adam and Josh all seemed to have discovered something interesting to inspect on their cans.

Connor looked at me. Josh's plan hadn't worked, so why not let Connor try? He's our year's technical genius, after all. And we used to be best mates, and I liked his gran . . .

'I'll come,' I said.

Ten

'And have you had your breakfast, lads?' said Connor's gran in her pink dressing gown as she set the big brown teapot on her kitchen table. 'Because this is a mighty early social call.'

I stared at the teapot. We had a teapot, but we only used it on special occasions like birthdays and Christmas. It was tea bags and mugs for us at home.

I yawned. Connor had woken me early by chucking little bits of gravel from our front path at my window. I was almost out of the door by the time Mum emerged and said, 'Where do you think you're going at this hour in the morning?'

'We're going to help get the disco ready,' I said truthfully.

'Publicity,' Connor added. 'It's our publicity campaign.'

'What about breakfast?'

I waved the last two chocolate digestives at Mum and ran. We'd made it in record time to Connor's gran's flat.

'Gran, you remember the bird box I made you last Christmas, the one you hung on your balcony?'

Connor's gran poured out two cups of tea as she said, 'Lovely piece of work, Connor. I had so much pleasure from that last spring. A couple of wrens nested there. There's me, eight floors up, and up and down the wrens flew all day long, first making the nest, then feeding the chicks. Oh, that was a lovely present, Connor.'

'Can I borrow it back?'

'Now why would you be wanting that?'

'It's ... it's a sort of experiment, Gran, to get publicity for our Christmas disco.'

'Your ma has told me all about the disco. It sounds a grand affair. A dancing man you'll be, Connor.'

'No, I'm not dancing. I'm responsible for the lighting. But, Gran, none of the girls from St Anne's want to come.'

Gran sat back in her chair and stared us up and down.

'And lovely lads like you,' she said at last. 'Hoity-toity, that's what girls are getting these days.'

'But I've got this idea to make them notice,' said Connor. 'We don't think they've seen the poster about the disco, so we've made a big hoarding.'

'Well, now, if it's the girls not knowing about it, that's soon put to rights. And my bird box will help?'

'I think it will, Gran. And no birds will be nesting in it in December.'

'You're right there, Connor, but bring it back. A beautiful present like that, I don't want it to go missing.'

Connor and I made our way round the little balcony. There was a stunning view over the town, but you had to keep your eyes down to avoid stepping on his gran's collection of shells, plants in old pots and painted tins, and the big cat tray. We unpinned the wooden nesting box from its hook on the wall. It had a door on a hinge at the back so that you could clean it out and a little hole at the front the right size for a bird but too small for a cat. I was impressed, but why Connor thought it would help the billboard, I couldn't fathom.

'And will it be one sausage or two you'll be having with your eggs?' called Connor's gran from her little kitchen.

The French test had started by the time we slipped into school.

Mr Bates looked up from the pile of papers he was marking and held his finger to his lips. All around us in the classroom heads were bent over paper, pencils were being chewed. Mr Bates tiptoed like some elderly ballet dancer out of the room, waving us into the passage, and shut the door.

'To be late on such a morning, *mes élèves*!' he said. 'The test is almost over.'

'Sorry, sir,' said Connor. 'We forgot.'

'Sir, Connor?'

'I mean, Monsieur.'

I'd forgotten all about French. I hadn't revised a thing. My memory's strange that way. I forget the things I hate doing and remember the things I like. There's got to be something wrong with it. Perhaps memory is next to the music bit in the brain and when Mum dropped me head first on the kitchen floor . . .

'And what sorry excuse do you have, Matthew?'

I looked at Mr Bates's ratty face. He's got this thin brown moustache running over his top lip and when he puts on his navy beret I think, there's a fake Frenchman.

'Sorry, Monsieur, but Connor and I have been detained on important publicity work for the Christmas disco.'

'I shall certainly have a word with Mr Grinston about this. We've never had a disco for first years before and if it interferes with the end of term tests . . . You boys will stay in at break to revise so you will not be able to discuss the test with the boys who have finished, and then you will take the test in your lunch hour.'

'But, Monsieur,' began Connor, 'we've got a meeting . . .'

'*Tant pis!*' said Mr Bates, which I thought sounded very rude but, when I looked it up in the dictionary at break, means *more's the pity*. I mean, how can I ever learn a foreign language if I don't even understand the English?

Adam organised our rescue in the lunch hour.

He's the sort who will only help if he can't find any

way of getting out of it, but if he's in sole charge, the boss, he loves it. No discussion for Adam, everyone has to do what he says or they're out.

His scrubbing-brush head bobbed up outside at the back of the classroom. I opened the window to let in a freezing rush of air.

'OK,' he said rapidly, 'there's four pages in the test and you have to write on all of them. Connor, you work on the first page. Matthew, you sit behind him, in front of the window, and pass out pages two and three through the window and Harry will work on them, and then Josh will copy out a second set.'

'What about page four?'

'You'll have to do that yourself, and then swap with Connor so he can copy it, and you can copy page one.'

When Mr Bates arrived in his ridiculous beret we were sitting ready, meek as lambs. He took his beret off, sniffed and stroked his moustache.

'*Fermez la fenêtre*, will you, Matthew? There's a howling gale in here.'

'*Fenêtre?*'

'Window, Matthew. You must have learned that in your primary school.'

There you are, it goes in one ear and out the other.

'Sorry, sir, I mean, Monsieur, but Connor's got a migraine and he'll pass out if he doesn't get any air.'

That's what happens to Mum when life gets too horrible for her, she goes and lies on her bed, clutching her head, with the curtains drawn.

73

'Migraine?' said Connor.

'Migraine?' said Mr Bates. 'Don't exaggerate, Matthew. It's probably a headache, a bit of worry about the test. Quite healthy in the circumstances.'

At the word headache, Connor clicked. I guess his mum doesn't get migraines. He held his head with both hands and gasped.

So the window was left open and it was freezing. First Mr Bates put his beret back on, then he pulled a scarf out of his pocket and wound it round his neck, then he said, 'Go on working quietly, boys. I shall be fetching a dictionary from the staff room.'

My fingers were numb round my pencil, but I collected Connor's pages two and three and thrust them, together with mine, into Adam's waving hand outside the window.

It's the one thing Harry's brilliant at, French. Must be all those shopping trips to Paris, or skiing in the Alps, or lazing around on the beaches near St Tropez where they don't wear too much. Or it could be the CDs from New York.

I tried to do page four as fast as I could and then swapped it for page one with Connor.

'Are you sure *pain* is the right word to circle under the picture of the doctor?' whispered Connor.

'Course it is,' I said. 'It's obvious, isn't it? *Pain*, that's what you're in when you go to the doctor.'

'But I thought it was the bakery, bread . . .'

The door opened and in marched Mr Bates.

'I said there was to be no talking.'

Four sheets of paper floated through the window.

'What's that? Did I see . . .'

I leaped to my feet. I couldn't believe Harry and Josh had finished them so quickly. I scrabbled on the floor for the sheets.

'I'll shut the window, sir . . . Monsieur. You're right, it is a gale, Monsieur, blowing all my work around. Here you are, and here's Connor's.'

'Bit of a muddle, aren't they?' said Mr Bates suspiciously. 'And I hope you've done a good job, because you certainly finished the test in record time. Matthew, I know you find French difficult. Do you want to check over the paper one last time?'

'No, Monsieur. It wasn't difficult at all.'

Mr Bates was suspicious all right, but I reckon he wanted to get back to the warm staff room and those mugs of steaming coffee that the teachers are all glued to when they answer the door.

'Thanks for the help, Harry,' I said as Connor and I joined the others in the playground.

'He only had to do the French,' said Adam. 'I masterminded it.'

'Course, Adam. It was a great plan.'

We couldn't risk Adam getting all sulky. He goes dangerously moody if he feels he's not getting 'proper respect'.

Connor rescued his gran's bird box from behind his

coat in the cloakroom and his Tesco bag with his hammer and nails. We grabbed our jackets and kicked a ball into the playground. When we got near the gate we threw the ball back in and slipped out.

By the time we reached the board on the side road to St Anne's we were puffed out. Connor nailed the bottom of the nesting box to the top of the board.

'It's going to need four of us to operate this,' he explained. 'Two to give extra support to the board from each side, one to stand further up the road and shout when a car is coming, and one to operate the speed camera.'

'Speed camera?' said four voices as we let the board drop in astonishment.

'Careful!' said Connor. 'You'll break off the camera.'

Adam pointed speechless at the nesting box sitting at the top of the board, Harry tossed back his shining mane and frowned, and I have to admit that Connor's mad genius had failed to get through to me.

'Look,' he said.

We held the board up again and Connor opened the little door at the back of the nesting box. He stuck the torch inside.

'Go and stand at the front,' he said. 'Watch.'

We stared at the nesting box, with its little hole for the birds to get in. Suddenly a brilliant light flashed through the hole and then went off. The torch.

None of us could think what to say, until Adam spoke for us all.

'Clever nut, aren't you, Connor? And what is that supposed to do?'

Connor's shock of ginger hair waved round the side of the nesting box. 'They'll slow down, all those cars and buses bringing the girls to school. They'll think it's a speed camera. And if they slow down they'll have time to read the board.'

We all stared at Connor. There's no doubt about it, we've got a proper Einstein at St David's.

Eleven

We didn't hang around after school. Connor, Adam, Josh and I had agreed to meet early the next morning to work the speed camera. It was no use including Harry, as he always came to school in the Jeep.

'I could ask my father to let me cycle in on my mountain bike, but I know he'll never let me.'

'Why not?' I said. 'What's the point of having a mountain bike like yours if you never use it?'

'Dad's afraid I might get mugged,' said Harry.

I can see what Harry's dad means. If I had Calvin Klein school trousers, a black leather school bag and a state-of-the-art mountain bike, *I* might get mugged. Being stinking rich is not all fun.

Still, things were looking up. Now that Connor had

abandoned Lego and was into lighting, he wasn't such a sad mate to have.

I hurried home alone in the deepening dark. There I was, humming a great song I'd heard on Kiss FM, trying out a bottom wiggle with my knees bent, when I went slap into something cold and dripping, hanging on the clothes line in our backyard.

Clothes line? We hardly ever use it now, as Mum's bought a drier with her new working riches.

In the light from the kitchen window I could see it was the mustard T-shirt and it looked smaller.

I went into the kitchen. There was Mum taking off her plastic apron and drying her hands.

'Mum, what's my new shirt doing all wet?'

'When I got back from work I took some clean laundry into your room and there was this funny smell.'

'Funny smell?'

'I think it came from the T-shirt on the chair. They sometimes treat cotton with a chemical to stiffen it, so I thought it wouldn't hurt to give it a quick wash.'

'Why's it on the line?'

'All this yellow colour came out in the water, so I thought we'd better let it dry naturally and not risk putting it in the drier.'

Mum was right. I wouldn't dare go near Amanda at the disco if my T-shirt ponged.

I sat down and dunked a tea bag in water from the kettle. I opened the biscuit tin and shook it upside down.

'It's no use making a point,' said Mum. 'Your friends cleaned us out of biscuits last weekend, not forgetting the last two you took for breakfast yesterday. If you have chocolate biscuits for breakfast, you can't expect to have them for tea as well.'

I licked a few miserable crumbs off the table.

'There's no need for such disgusting behaviour,' said Mum sharply.

'Finished the biscuits, has he?' came Amy's voice as she opened the door.

She tottered in like some drunk thrown out of the pub on a Saturday night. I know about them because there's a pub up the road and the drunks stagger past, beneath my bedroom window, waking me up with their laughing and singing.

Amy toppled forward and clutched the edge of the table. I grabbed my mug as it tilted dangerously.

'You're drunk,' I said.

'Drunk . . . How cheeky can you be!' she gasped, putting her hands down to each foot in turn. 'Look!'

Amy placed on the table, spearing the few remaining biscuit crumbs, two purple shoes with the highest, sharpest heels I'd ever seen.

'Amy!' said Mum. 'How can you walk in those?'

'She can't,' I said.

'Mum let me buy them in the end, because I told her you didn't mind.'

'But you said you were only going to wear them on Saturday night.'

'I am, but I've got to practise walking in them, haven't I? I'll wear them properly on Saturday night when I go out. Don't you like them, Aunty Sue? They cost me all my savings.'

'I didn't think they'd be that high,' said Mum anxiously. 'You could twist an ankle easily on those. Pretty colour, though.'

'Talking of colour,' said Amy, sinking down on a chair between me and Mum, 'that's a disgusting-coloured shirt slapped me on the face as I came in. Men, isn't it? They just don't know what suits. My dad's the same. He wears some ghastly stuff.'

It felt as if Amy had stabbed one of her spiky heels into my chest. I couldn't breathe. Mum went pink and flustered and leaped about, pretending to look for cheese crackers.

'So what are you planning for Saturday night, Amy?' said Mum quickly.

'What's wrong with that shirt?' I breathed out at last.

'We're going to meet at Suzy's house,' Amy burbled on. 'Then we're going to see the new James Bond. What are you going on about, Matty? That shirt. Well, don't tell Uncle Simon I said so, but it's revolting. I mean, what a dreadful colour . . . It's like sick. Nobody looks good in dirty yellow.'

'It's mustard yellow.'

'I can see that. Not English mustard, but that browny, yellow French mustard. Dirty yellow, like I said.'

Amy stared at me for a moment, then put her hand

to her strawberry mouth and collapsed in peals of laughter.

'Don't tell me it's yours,' she shrieked.

'It's for the disco,' said Mum helpfully.

The laughter was wiped off Amy's face. She looked shocked.

'For the disco?' she said. 'But you can't wear that, Matty. You'll be a laughing stock.'

'Well, he's going to have to,' said Mum firmly. 'He chose it, so he can wear it.'

After James had been dragged yelling from the lounge to bed, Mum and Dad settled themselves in front of the telly. The only place left for me to be alone was the kitchen. I kept reading and reading my history book, but none of it went in. Later I tossed and turned in my bunk above James, trying to get to sleep.

I couldn't go to that disco now. I wasn't going to be seen dead there.

But I couldn't let Connor and Adam and Harry and Josh down either.

It was getting light and I swear I hadn't slept a wink when my alarm woke me. I had to help with the speed camera.

'Any tests today?' said Dad as he tossed a charred piece of toast on my plate.

'Dunno,' I said wearily.

'Dunno?' said Dad. 'That just isn't good enough, Matthew. It's your business to know. You should have a more positive attitude to school. Living outside the catchment area, we're dead lucky you got into St David's. I had to do a lot of pushing on your behalf. "Dunno" is not good enough.'

This is Dynamic Dad. He strikes occasionally at breakfast, but fortunately fizzles out by teatime.

'You've got to seize your opportunities in life, exploit them to the full, and a good school is your first great opportunity.'

I dragged my sports kit out of the cupboard and headed for the door.

'You've forgotten your school bag,' yelled Dad after me. 'Wake up, Matthew. There's a life out there.'

Not for me, there wasn't.

When Dad saw my test results he'd be so dynamic he'd blow us both up.

And discos . . . I could only dance a little bit and I couldn't choose good clothes. I didn't mind if no girl from St Anne's looked at me, but I'd die if they laughed at me.

Mustard yellow.

I was never going near that stall in the market again. I'd tell all my friends not to shop there and hope that black-leather-jacketed creep went broke.

Twelve

The grey light was brightening as I plodded down the main road. By the time I turned off down the side road to St Anne's, a bright sun was rising over the golf course.

Connor was fiddling with the speed camera. I noticed a second pair of legs under the board, and they wore black suede shoes with thick crêpe soles, the sort that Mum refuses to let me have.

'Josh, you here already?'

'Came early with Connor,' was the muffled voice from behind the board.

'Don't let go, Josh,' shouted Connor. 'I've nearly got it set up.'

It's a strange world. I seemed to spend most of my time trying to keep Connor away from Josh, because

84

he's such a major embarrassment, and here they were arriving together.

'Matthew, you take over from Josh and give him a break,' said Connor bossily.

I went round the back, and there was Josh propping up the board with his shoulder.

They seemed to have it all sewn up. I took over the board. I couldn't see too much with it just centimetres from my nose.

Adam arrived when Connor had finished setting us all up.

'You're late,' Connor complained. 'You should have been here to help.'

'Been spying out the lane,' said Adam. 'I'm going to stand on the bend. When I see a car coming I'll signal back like this.'

He gave an ear-splitting whistle before he ran back to take up his position.

'Look, that's the first car,' said Josh, and there was something unusually like excitement in his voice.

'Prop up the board, Matthew,' yelled Connor. 'You, Josh, push from your side. I'll just climb up . . .'

Connor pulled his torch out of a Tesco bag and leaped up onto the camping stool he had brought with him.

'Got it!' said Connor, as the torch flashed on and off.

Whistle after piercing whistle rang down from the corner.

'Go on,' shouted Josh. 'That's right, keep flashing. This big red one coming . . . it's crammed with girls.'

The cars were streaming past now. I peered round the edge of the board and watched the faces of the drivers. There were some mums with tangly hair, looking as if they had just got out of bed, and others with bright lipstick in place, dropping the girls off on their way to work. Some dads were in overalls and others in suits. But were they looking, reading the notice?

'Connor, they're not reading the notice.'

'What do you mean, Matthew?'

'They see the light, then they slow down all right, but they stare straight ahead, as if they've got a stiff neck or something.'

I suddenly remembered what happens when Dad passes a speed camera. We see the light flash at the car ahead and shout, 'Camera!' Dad brakes and we sit very still, staring ahead, hoping the camera is not going to catch us. It's almost as if we think the camera won't see us if we don't look at it.

'Matthew's right,' confirmed Josh. 'They're staring straight ahead . . . terrified.'

Suddenly the board wobbled backwards. I tried to grab it, but it banged against my nose before collapsing on the verge.

'Josh, you let go!' yelled Connor.

'There's no point if they're not looking,' said Josh.

Adam came running down the road. 'What are you lot doing? There are streams of cars still coming. Look, if you've been having a fight, Matthew . . .'

'I've been holding the board up,' I said. 'You think that everyone is fighting just because . . .'

'Well, look at your nose,' said Adam.

I couldn't look, but I gingerly felt it with a hand that came away bloody.

'Let's give up,' I said. 'It's a crazy idea and it's not going to work.'

'Just in time for the history test,' said Mr Smallman-Smith, as we slunk into the history room. 'Harry here was just telling me you four all had a nasty virus and were visiting the doctor.'

Behind Mr Smallman-Smith, Harry was mouthing something incomprehensible and clutching his throat.

I coughed. Josh and Adam got the message and joined in.

'No, I'm fine,' began Connor, but I stepped on his foot and pressed until he got the message too.

Maybe Mum's right and there are some advantages to sensible leather uppers over trendy trainers. The trouble with Connor is he's never been able to spot a lie and so he's no good at telling one.

'Your coughs seem to have abated, so I think we are ready to start the test. Matthew, you hand out the papers.'

It had been a miserable night and a miserable morning, so why not a miserable test as well?

In history we've done the Civil War this term, all the gory stuff with Charles I getting his head cut off. When

Mr Smallman–Smith asked us if we would have been a Cavalier and fought for the king or a Roundhead and fought for Parliament and the rights of the people, we all said Cavaliers. I mean, they had the best fancy clothes and a handsome, brave leader, Prince Rupert, while that old Oliver Cromwell, who led the Roundheads, had a pimple on his nose.

When I looked at the test there was some sort of document we had to explain: . . . *no maids are to be decked with gaudy ribbons, and there is to be no dancing round the MayPole, and no music but godly hymns shall be heard . . .*

It's obvious. It's about the Puritans, and Oliver Cromwell was a Puritan and they didn't like dancing.

So I'm changing my mind. I'm backing the Roundheads from now on.

Thirteen

My tummy rumbled through most of the test. I was starving. I'd been in such a hurry to get out to operate the speed camera that I'd barely nibbled Dad's charred toast.

'Chippy?' I whispered to Josh as I handed in our test papers.

'Sounds good,' agreed Josh.

At lunch we slipped out of the gates as fast as we could, praying that no one would notice. Once outside, I exploded.

'I've had enough of this disco rubbish,' I yelled. 'The St Anne's girls don't like us, they don't want to come and that's fine by me.'

Josh shrugged.

'We're at the wrong school, Josh. I mean, St David's is ancient . . . It's like a museum. We should have gone to

Woodside Park. I'm in the catchment area and they have girls as well, and they wear what they like to school.'

Josh nodded wisely.

'If they have girls already at Woodside Park, they wouldn't have to persuade them to buy tickets for a disco. If they're anything like my cousin Amy, they'd be organising the whole thing and marching in the boys at gunpoint.'

Josh gurgled, like he was swallowing a chuckle.

I was encouraged.

'It's my parents' fault. It's exams, exams, exams . . . Just because St David's is supposed to have this fantastic reputation with exam results. They don't know what's going to hit them, because my test results are going to be—'

There was an old lady waiting at a bus stop and glaring at me, so I didn't say what I was going to say.

'And this disco is the end of the line. I'm going to have nothing more to do with it. Who likes the St Anne's girls anyway? I bet St Anne's is a dump too, and the only real girls are at Woodside Park.'

'I could hear your voice way down the road,' said Connor, tapping me on the shoulder. 'You're shouting.'

'Who asked you?' I yelled at Connor.

Connor's eyes opened wide with surprise. 'Do I have to ask before I speak?'

'Yes, you do, if it's anything to do with that disco and your stupid speed camera.'

'I thought it was a good idea,' said Connor lamely.

It was a brilliant idea, I knew that. It just hadn't worked.

I had been raving and shouting, but it wasn't Connor's fault. I did wish that he wouldn't keep trailing me.

'Shall we get some chips, Josh?' said Connor.

'That's what we've come for,' said Josh.

'I can smell them from here,' said Connor. 'Cor!' He bent double and groaned. 'It's agony.'

We all three broke into a run, pushing each other out of the way to get to the chip shop first. I won.

It occurred to me then that Josh liked Connor. Maybe I didn't have to worry so much about him tagging along and looking embarrassing.

At least that was one less thing to worry about.

I watched Mrs Andropoulis shake the chips out of the basket, fill three paper bags to the top, douse them in vinegar and sprinkle them with salt.

We leaned against the wall outside to eat them, because when I've eaten the first layer I like to nip back inside and shake more vinegar on the second.

It was freezing eating outside. The wind was whistling down the road and I swear it came straight from Siberia. Old leaves, litter, plastic bags and pages from a freebie newspaper some paperboy must have dropped scuttled past us, clinging to our legs.

Josh leaned down to unwrap a sheet of newspaper from around his black suede shoes. He picked it up.

'What do you want with that?' said Connor. 'It's no good for sport.'

'Just looking at the gigs.'

'The gigs?' I said.

'Music,' sighed Josh.

I wasn't too sure even then what a gig was, so I peered over Josh's shoulder as he turned the pages.

'Stop!' I cried. 'Turn back to that last page. Look.'

I thought I'd seen 'St Anne's'! There it was. A big notice taking up a quarter of the page:

ST ANNE'S OPEN DAY, FRIDAY, 9 DECEMBER

All parents of prospective pupils for St Anne's are cordially invited to our open day on Friday 9 December. Please call 0683 4598 for a copy of our prospectus and to make an appointment to view the school. We will be proud to show you round and look forward to meeting your daughters.

'Look at that,' I cried, stabbing the newspaper.

'It's this Friday,' said Josh.

'We can sneak into St Anne's,' grinned Connor. 'And leave the notice in the playground.'

'Don't be a nut, Connor,' I said. 'It's not for brothers. It's for daughters and their parents.'

We looked at each other and I swear the penny dropped in each of our heads at the same time.

'Don't be daft,' grinned Josh.

I'm not sure I'd seen Josh grin before.

'Play-acting's not my sort of thing,' said Connor. 'Now if I could pretend to be an engineer and get in to mend the lights . . .'

'You're too small, Connor,' I said brutally. 'You'd never look like a grown-up engineer. You're going to have to be a girl.'

Connor's eyes threatened to pop out of his head.

'A girl?'

'Yeah. You're going to have to be the "prospective pupil" and, I suppose . . .' I sized Josh up and down. Yes, he was definitely a lot taller than me. 'I suppose you're going to have to be the father, Josh.'

Josh smirked happily. 'So you're going to have to be mother.'

I nodded. But I didn't like it one bit.

I sat through the technology revision lesson without taking in a word.

I'd got carried away with my idea for infiltrating St Anne's. I'd been shouting and raving and sort of showing off. But Josh's billboard hadn't worked, nor had Connor's bird box/speed camera, so why not go through with my idea for the open day?

But it was a mad scheme. Totally – utterly – mad.

In the cloakroom at the end of the afternoon, Josh sidled up and nudged me. 'We've only got two days. I'll get my outfit ready and make some flyers.'

'Flyers?'

'I told you what they were before. Leaflets about the disco. Publicity about the venue. We'll leave little piles of them in each classroom when they show us round. What are you going to wear? I mean, I'm going to look good and I don't want an ugly wife.'

I didn't know what had got into Josh. He'd never said so much in his life before.

'I don't know. What do mothers wear? I'll have a look through Mum's cupboards.'

When I got home it was Dad's turn to be back from work first, although I could hardly see him in the kitchen for the smoke.

'Burnt the sausages again?' I said.

'What do you mean "again"? I've only tried to cook them once before.'

'I don't like them burnt,' wailed James.

'Well, mate, you're going to have to eat them or starve,' said Dad, and even James knew to keep quiet.

We didn't see the door open, but we felt the blast of air.

'Your mother can take over,' said Dad with relief.

But it wasn't Mum. It was Amy.

She sniffed the air. 'Mmm,' she said. 'I love burnt sausages.'

I grabbed the frying pan, I wasn't going to have Amy guzzling my sausages, burnt or not.

'Ow!' The pan dropped to the floor.

'Are you trying to help or something?' yelled Dad.

'It's hot.'

'Of course it's hot, or don't they teach you that in science? You need heat if you're going to burn anything. I don't think you're getting down to this revision properly, Matthew. At your age I would have given my right hand to have the opportunities you young people have. You take it all for granted and fling it on the floor . . .'

I couldn't quite follow Dad's reasoning, but I knew he was trying to blame me for the sausages.

Amy watched with interest as she gnawed at a black sausage.

'And don't *you* offer to help,' said Dad to Amy, 'or you might fall off those ridiculous shoes.'

'Too many cooks spoil the broth,' said Amy. 'And these days men should be able to cook. Anyway, I didn't come to have supper. I came to see Matthew.'

Amy elbowed me out of the kitchen and tottered into the sitting room.

'I thought Aunty Sue wouldn't be here tonight, that's why I came. Look, see what I've got you.'

I stared at the scrap of black lacy stuff she pushed into my hand. Then I picked it up between my thumb and first finger. It was . . . gulp! . . . yes, it was . . . some black lacy pants. Pretty small . . . not much of them . . . but definitely a pair of lady's black lacy knickers.

'I thought they'd be a good idea,' she whispered.

How had she known? Surely I didn't need those.

Who was going to look at what I was wearing underneath my clothes?

The key rattled in the front door.

'Quick, hide them. Keep them for the end of the week and I'll be round.'

I stuffed them in my trouser pocket as Mum marched through the front door.

'My God! What's this smoke? Can't I even trust you to cook a sausage supper, Simon?'

Fourteen

Clothes . . . I hate clothes.

I hate shopping trips with Mum, I hate it when I get dumped with a sicky T-shirt and I hate those scratchy black lace pants.

There I was, standing in front of the mirror in Mum and Dad's bedroom, while Mum was making a scene downstairs in the kitchen, preparing herself a 'healthy' salad.

'Any more of these unhealthy meals, Simon, and we shall have malnourished children on our hands.'

'They get good school dinners, Sue,' came Dad's voice. 'Or why else am I shelling out the money for them?'

'Pizzas, sausages . . . It's not a diet for growing children.'

'Come off it, Sue. I grew up on chips, tea and jam butties.'

I shut the door of the bedroom. I reckoned I had quarter of an hour of safe searching before they left the kitchen.

What did mothers wear on a school visit? Mum had her second suit for work in the cupboard, but I was not going to be seen dead in a skirt.

Trousers? They all looked a funny shape to me. If I was going to wear trousers, I could wear my own. My black tracksuit bottoms, for instance. Lots of women wear tracksuits.

But what about the lacy pants? Nobody was going to look under the tracksuit bottoms, I hoped, so why did Amy think I had to wear lacy pants as well?

I held out the pants and stretched them across my school trousers. Hopeless. There was no way I was going to fit all my bits in them. Another of Amy's rubbish suggestions.

I crept out of the bedroom and across to James's and my room. James was mucking around on the computer.

'What's that?'

'What?'

'You're hiding something. Show me.'

'I'm not,' I said as I stuffed the black pants down behind the computer.

Nobody bothered to dust there. In fact nobody dusts much at all in our house any longer.

I was contemplating whether I had time to creep

back into Mum's bedroom and find something to wear for the top half of the tracksuit when on the landing I heard . . .

'And the dustbin isn't out, Simon. Tomorrow is rubbish day. Do I have to work from nine to five and still carry out every little chore in this house?'

'I was going to do it, Sue, but I've only just finished scraping off the burnt bits in the frying pan. And *I've* been toiling away at work today too. Do I have to come back from the office and set to with the Brillo Pad all evening?'

'You burnt the sausages.'

There was a pause, as if Dad couldn't think of a good answer. It's often like that. Mum's comments strike like lightning flashes.

'What have I got a strapping lad for? At his age I was doing all the chores. Matthew!' An ear-splitting shout echoed up the stairs. 'Matthew . . . come down this minute.'

'He's got to revise,' said Mum. 'He's got his techno-logy test tomorrow.'

Technology! I'd forgotten all about it.

'Mum's right. I've got to revise, Dad,' I shouted down the stairs, my voice cracked with panic.

'Five minutes spent putting the dustbin out on the street isn't going to make much difference. A bit of cold air will wake you up.'

As I dragged the dustbin outside, I thought of the lacy pants behind the computer. I should have kept them in my pocket, then I could have chucked them in the dustbin. Too late now.

I scooted James out of our bedroom and spread my technology book out on the table. There was the diagram of an electric circuit, all pluses and minuses. I'd built it with Connor and he'd done it all, while I drew cartoons with Josh. I wished now I'd helped Connor.

The phone rang for ages downstairs in the living room. Mum and Dad were shouting about who should get it. How could I revise with parents like mine, who never stopped bickering?

I clapped my hands over my ears.

The door was flung open. It was Mum, eyes glinting and hair all over the place.

'It's for you, Matthew. Perhaps you can answer the phone for once.'

'I'm revising. You said—'

'Do I have to stand here all evening or are you coming down?'

It was Connor.

'You've saved my life, Connor. I don't remember a thing about that electric circuit we built.'

'It's easy. Think it through. I've—'

'I have thought it through and it doesn't make sense.'

'OK. We'll get in early to school and I'll go through it with you.'

'Thanks, Connor.' Now I felt guilty about all the

times I'd tried to get rid of him. Only a real mate puts himself out for you like that.

'Matthew, it's the clothes.'

'What's up?'

'All their clothes are in their bedroom,' Connor gabbled down the line, 'and they notice immediately if any of them has borrowed from the other without asking . . . And even if I sneak some, my sisters are both a lot bigger than me. I really don't want to be a girl, Matthew.'

Too right, I thought, I don't want to be a mother either.

'I'll give Josh a ring,' I said. 'Perhaps this isn't such a good idea after all.'

'Course we're not giving up,' Josh said. 'I've got my outfit all ready. This was your great idea, so you should see it through.'

I couldn't believe this. Josh was even beginning to sound like a dad. Perhaps that was what came of playing grown-ups . . . you found yourself really acting the part. Like Mum, I'd start yelling about the state of the kitchen soon.

'Connor, I've spoken to Josh.'

'Yes?'

'We're going ahead.'

'Where am I going to get some girl's clothes that don't make me look like a midget?'

I thought, and then it came to me.

'Have you taken the bird box back to your gran yet?'

'No, I was going to at the weekend.'

'Take it back before school tomorrow and get your gran to help. Say it's . . . it's for a play you're in at school. She's tiny, your gran. She can't be any bigger than you.'

There was a deathly silence from the phone.

'I'm not tiny,' came Connor's wounded voice at last.

'No, course not,' I said hastily. 'But your gran's tiny for a grown-up.'

'Well, how will I have time to get to Gran's and teach you about the electric circuit before school starts?'

'You'll have to get up extra early. Borrow an alarm clock.'

So I *was* beginning to sound like a mum.

And then Dad invaded my privacy yet again.

'I hope this isn't our call. The telephone bill is big enough as it is. Who have you been phoning?'

'Josh and Connor.'

'Two calls! That's going to cost a bit. I thought you were meant to be revising your technology.'

'Mum spends hours on the phone to Aunty Eileen,' I said.

'None of your lip, lad,' said Dad. 'Get back up to that revision.'

That was the odd thing about my parents. They were always yelling at each other, but if I said one critical word about either of them, the other leaped to their defence.

Then they surprised me. After James went to bed, they went out to the pub for a drink, leaving me in charge.

'We'll be back by nine,' Dad said cheerfully.

It was heaven-sent. I ransacked Mum's drawers and wardrobe. I found a pink fluffy jumper and an orange silky scarf. Mum had liked the red and orange T-shirt in the market, so I reckoned this was the sort of thing she wore. I didn't dare take her winter coat, because she's only got the one and she might have wanted it, so I found a pale blue jacket she wears in summer, with a frilly bit down the front.

My hair. It was too boyish. I'd have to cover it with a hat. There was a green woolly hat at the back of one drawer with a flowery pom-pom thing on the side. Dad had given it to Mum last Christmas, but I don't think she's ever worn it. Come to think of it . . . I don't think Mum ever wears green.

I pulled it over my head. It came down low, like an upside-down yoghurt pot, with the flowery pom-pom between my ear and my cheek. I stuffed the clothes into a plastic bag and then wedged them into the bottom of my school bag.

I was going to have to hide that lot at school until Friday and the St Anne's open day.

Fifteen

I didn't want to talk to anyone about the technology test. I'm bad at English, but at least you can waffle on and hope for the best. With technology, you either know it or you don't.

I didn't.

It wasn't made any easier by Dad going on, all Thursday evening, about the future being technology.

'Technology, IT, computers . . . Matthew, that's where the jobs are going to be. Well-paid, fortunes made in a few years. Why, there's lads scarcely older than you driving around in Ferraris. IT wizards. Oh, yes, if I was starting again, I'd be into technology.'

That got me, because I'd die for a Ferrari. But as I am not going to make it in technology, and no one is going to want give an exam pooper a job, it looks like

I shall have to go on living without one.

So there we were, Friday lunchtime, Josh and me and Connor, creeping behind the caretaker's house, where there's a gap between the side of the house and the school wall, carrying bulging plastic bags.

Connor and I were grimly silent, but Josh was humming away.

'Shut up, Josh,' I whispered. 'We don't want anyone to hear us.'

I stripped off my school shirt, sweater, trousers and shoes, until I was down to my underpants. It was freezing! Have you ever tried stripping off outside, in mid-December? I pulled the black tracksuit bottoms on and struggled to get the pink sweater over my head. It was scratchy next to my skin. What mums have to put up with, wearing clothes like that . . . I pulled on the frilly blue jacket next. It was dead itchy . . . and wasn't warm at all. I was going to freeze.

I flipped the flimsy orange scarf this way and that but it wouldn't stay on, so I tied it in a knot.

Shoes? I hadn't thought of shoes. I'd have to wear my black leather school lace-ups, because I certainly wasn't going barefoot.

I was glad of the green yoghurt-pot hat. I can't think why Mum hasn't worn it, because it's quite warm.

Done!

I turned round and looked at Josh.

He looked fantastic! Dark suit with wide gangster stripes, navy shirt, a shimmery cream tie with . . . with

. . . mermaids on, all silvery tails and, well, not too much on the top. Good thing they don't feel the cold.

He took a comb out of his pocket and a pot of some greasy-looking stuff, spread the grease over his palms and then rubbed it through his hair. Then he combed his hair straight up and put on his designer specs.

I tell you, he looked at least eighteen, although the trousers were quite a bit too long over his shoes, and his jacket seemed to come down to his knees.

'Wow, Josh!' I said. 'You look great. What about me?'

Josh surveyed me up and down for a long time.

'Mm,' he said without much enthusiasm. 'My brothers would never go out with a girl who wore school shoes with tracksuit bottoms. You could have worn your trainers.'

'I didn't think,' I said miserably.

'And your colour coordination is wrong. Pink and orange and pale blue. I'm not sure it's going to go with the lipstick.'

'Lip . . . lipstick?' The cold was getting to me and my teeth were chattering.

'Here. It's a special occasion, visiting a school. Got to look as if you've made an effort. Put this on.'

Josh fished a gold tube out of his pocket. He pulled off the top and twiddled the bottom, and up came a stub of red lipstick.

'Where'd you get that?' I muttered.

'Some girlfriend left it at our house. Here, take it.'

'I'm ready,' said Connor behind us. Connor's voice

was flat and dull, as if someone had squeezed out all its usual bounce.

Josh and I turned round and . . . stared.

Connor looked just like a real girl with ginger curly hair. He was wearing a blue flowery dress with a white woolly cardigan, and on his feet he wore white ankle socks and black shiny shoes with a bar strap across the front. Amy had worn clothes like that when Aunty Eileen dressed her up for parties when she was little.

'Don't say anything,' said Connor gloomily. 'I don't want to know.'

'But, Connor,' said Josh, 'you look great! No one will know you're not a girl.'

'Are those your gran's clothes?' I asked. I'd never seen his gran in anything but trousers.

'No. They're clothes my mum wore when she was a girl for church. Gran kept them as a souvenir or something. I've got to look after them. The shoes are too tight. They're agony and I'm freezing.'

Poor Connor. I couldn't complain.

'Better get over the wall,' said Josh. 'Hey, Matthew. Put your lipstick on.'

'How?'

'Look into that window. It's so dark down here that it's as good as a mirror.'

I leaned forward towards the window and smeared the stuff across my lips. I could see it was a bit smudged in the corners, so I peered closer and rubbed a finger across my bottom lip. But instead of seeing my lip reflected back I was staring into a pair of glaring eyes. Funny ... my eyes are blue, like Mum's. These were dark brown and they were wide with surprise.

'Quick! We've gotta get out of here,' I whispered hoarsely. 'There's someone in there and they've seen me.'

I dropped the lipstick and we hauled ourselves up and scrambled over the wall.

Sixteen

We joined the stream of parents and little girls heading for the main steps of St Anne's.

'I can't keep up with you two,' whispered Connor. 'These shoes are killing me.'

'Slow down, Matthew,' said Josh. 'You're striding out. Mothers in their best clothes don't stride out.'

I was nervous. I wanted to get this over as soon as possible.

Inside the door a skinny teacher in navy blue sat at a desk, checking each family off against a list.

'Delighted to see you, Mr and Mrs Turner, and this of course must be Rachel.'

The teacher leaned forward to give Rachel a toothy smile.

'And what's your favourite subject, dear? Writing

stories? You must go and see our lovely library.'

Mr Turner neatened his tie and beamed down at his daughter.

Then the teacher asked a girl in St Anne's uniform to show the Turner family round the school. As she stepped forward from the clutch of girls chatting beside the door, I froze. It was Zoe. I knew it was Zoe. I ducked my head down.

She'd grown and her brown curly hair was long and tied back in a bunch. She looked a lot older, but you can't forget the girl you played toy farms with for most of your childhood.

I could hear the girls giggling. What were they giggling at?

'Girls,' hissed the teacher, 'remember, it's our very best behaviour.'

Then she saw Josh and her mouth fell open. She tried to speak, but, strangely for a teacher, she didn't seem to be able to find anything to say.

'Can . . . can I help you?' she spluttered at last.

She stared at the mermaids as if she was hypnotised.

'Mr and Mrs Sam Featherstonehaugh III.'

Josh was speaking in a ridiculous American accent which made him sound like the worst actor in some old movie on Sunday afternoon telly.

The teacher took a deep breath and pulled herself stiffly upright in her chair.

'Your name isn't on the list,' she said firmly. 'You haven't made an appointment.'

Josh didn't look cool any longer. He stood there shifting from one foot to another. He must have rehearsed the line for his entrance, but beyond that he was lost, and we had forgotten about needing an appointment.

'Oh, damn,' I tried. 'I did phone, but I must have spoken to the wrong person.'

The teacher's head jerked over to me and she screwed up her eyes in a suspicious way I didn't like. It was probably my lipstick. I'd smudged it when we left school in such a hurry. She hesitated, as if she couldn't quite make up her mind, then said, 'I thought for a moment you were an American family. How silly of me. Well, we are a bit tight tonight, so I don't think we can show . . . who is this girl?'

The sight of Connor seemed to surprise her. She leaned across the table.

'He's . . . she's Anastasia,' said Josh, back on track.

'Anastasia,' murmured the teacher. She smiled at Connor. 'Tell me, Anastasia, dear, what do you most enjoy at school.'

Connor gulped and stared at me. I kicked him on the ankle.

'Maths, technology, anything electrical, lighting systems, general science, mending old cars . . .'

The teacher sat back in her chair and stared at Connor. Her smile was twisting before our eyes. It seemed to go up at one side and down on the other. Mr Grinston can do that too, when he's being sarcastic.

111

'How very impressive,' said the teacher, staring at Connor's flowered dress. 'And how refreshing to find such advanced scientific and practical interests in such . . . such a pretty young girl.'

Connor's head drooped in despair.

'Stephanie, it's your turn, isn't it?' A tubby girl was hanging back, trying to hide behind another girl. 'Come along now, Stephanie! I don't think Mr and Mrs Featherstonehaugh will need the full tour, as they haven't an appointment.'

She whispered intently in Stephanie's ear, and I caught something about 'the back door', but the teacher didn't have time to finish whatever it was she wanted to explain, because two parents, both carrying identical black briefcases, leaned impatiently over her table.

'Dr Peter Welkinsop and Dr Sarah Welkinsop,' said the father, as both he and his wife put their big cases with a thud on the floor, 'and this of course is our daughter, Kate Welkinsop.'

The teacher became all flustered and went pink with pleasure. 'Drs Welkinsop, we are delighted to welcome you. What is it, Stephanie? Just get Mr and Mrs Featherstonehaugh away,' and then I'm sure she hissed, under her breath, 'out of sight'.

Josh seemed to recover himself and looked furious.

'We want the full tour,' he announced to the sulky Stephanie.

He marched ahead, following Mr and Mrs Turner and Rachel into the first classroom.

Stephanie muttered, 'This is the geography room,' and retreated as far from us as was possible without going back out of the door.

Other parents were looking at the display on global warming on the wall, but when they saw us they stared and seemed more interested in us than in the wall display.

One mother put her hand to her mouth, but I could see she was laughing.

'Josh,' I whispered, 'put those flyers on that table by the door. Let's get moving, because I'm not staying here too long.'

Josh felt in the deep pocket of his suit jacket, first one side and then the other. Then he plunged his hands so hard into his trouser pockets that the trousers nearly came down. He yanked them back up and turned a face more ghostly than any I've yet seen on Josh.

'I haven't got them.'

'What do you mean, you haven't got them! You've got to have them. That's why we're here.'

'I don't know. Perhaps they fell out of my pockets when we climbed over the wall.'

'Fell . . . out . . . of . . . your . . . pockets,' I hissed. 'You idiot! You plonker! You halfwit!'

I'd got dressed in all that fluffy, scratchy, freezing fancy dress for nothing.

'Come on,' said Stephanie sullenly. 'We've got to keep going. It's the music room next, then the hall, the gym, the computer room . . .'

What could we do? We had to keep going. Connor was limping along behind in his shiny black shoes. Josh was desperately searching his jacket pockets, so I strode out and led the way, pushing Stephanie on as fast as I could.

'Any questions?' Stephanie asked in a bored voice.

'No, thanks,' I said fiercely.

We were coming out of the hall, down the passageway to the entrance again. Parents seemed to flatten themselves against walls as we passed, and little girls clutched at their mother's hands.

'Look at that,' came Connor's pained voice from behind.

'We've seen enough,' I said sternly.

'No stop, Matthew, look at that board.'

As soon as Connor said 'Matthew', Stephanie stopped and stared at me, and began giggling. Ahead of her I thought I saw Zoe turn and look back.

I turned, to urge Connor to stagger the last few metres to the door and freedom, when it caught my eye too.

'Josh – er, I mean Sam – come back. Look at that!'

It was a notice board of events. Pinned in the centre was a homemade poster of a couple dancing. The lady, in a dress with a frill at the bottom, was daintily kicking out her feet and twirling her long pearl necklace with one hand. The man was dancing with his knees bent, but what was odd was his arms. They were straight down beside his sides, with the hands sticking out flat.

His hair was slicked back and he was wearing a suit with a spotted bow tie.

COME AND CHARLESTON WITH US
BE A BRIGHT YOUNG THING
BE THE BELLE OF THE BALL!

St David's first years invite St Anne's first years to their Christmas Disco on 16 December at 7 p.m. Tickets are available from Mr Grinston, Head of Year Seven, St David's.

'What on earth is that?' I said.

Stephanie came alive at last and inspected the poster.

'It's awful, isn't it?' she giggled. 'I mean, it's like out of a history book. Course, none of us are going.'

Josh looked utterly confused. 'Charleston? What's that?'

'I know,' said Connor. 'My gran can charleston, my great-gran taught her. She's really good. It's an ancient dance.'

'When was that trendy?'

'Before the Second World War.'

'Cor!' said Josh. 'Grinston's old, but I never guessed he was as old as that.'

'What are you doing?' cried Stephanie.

'I'm taking it with me,' I said, as I took the pins out of the poster. 'I'm not having Anastasia going to a disco like that.'

'Stephanie . . . Stephanie!' A familiar voice echoed down the corridor. 'I said the back door. Get them out . . .' The teacher's voice was rising to a shriek. Then it dropped suddenly to a gushy, 'Yes, indeed. We have a very high standard of artwork at St Anne's.'

'Not this poster,' I muttered. 'This is rubbish.'

Outside the front door, Connor pulled off the black shoes and we pelted across to the gate.

I wasn't sure, but I thought I heard a voice call 'Matthew' from behind. In any case, I wasn't stopping to look.

Seventeen

It was Saturday, so it wasn't easy getting everyone together and finding a place to meet where no one would listen in.

'My parents are having forty people over for a buffet supper tonight,' said Harry when I called him, because I reckoned he had the biggest house and he must have some quiet, out-of-the-way rooms. 'The florist is decorating the downstairs room and the hall, and the caterers are in the kitchen, and the beautician is here upstairs painting my mother's nails, and my father has taken over my computer. He's trying to contact his trader in Tokyo.'

'Well, what are *you* doing?' I asked Harry.

'Sitting on the stairs. Can I come round to your house?'

It was crazy. Our matchbox would barely cover a quarter of his front lawn and Harry had to come round to our house to find a place to talk.

'No,' I said. 'If you think you can get peace and quiet in this place, think again.' I didn't like to say it, but what with Mum and Dad constantly at war and James whining to get attention, there was one thing our house was not good for . . . and that was providing a bit of quiet thinking space to solve a big problem.

Connor's mum said we were welcome at theirs provided we kept quiet while Connor's dad watched the football, and if we didn't bother Connor's sisters, who were washing their hair for the youth club party that evening.

It was all right for those who could idle Saturday afternoons away watching football and washing their hair . . .

When I asked for Josh, a big brother said, 'He's out,' and put the phone down. I was beginning to think that grown-up brothers aren't all they're cracked up to be. Except that I'm one, of course.

Then Connor rang back.

'We can go to my gran's. She loves visitors and she can keep a secret, and I bet she'll let us have her living room to ourselves.'

When I called Harry back, he asked, 'Isn't that the rough estate next to the London Road?'

I rang Josh again and tried to leave directions and a message. 'Yup,' said his brother and put the phone down again. So I wasn't convinced we were going to see either Josh or Harry.

We met at three at Connor's gran's flat. Josh was waiting for me at the foot of the stairwell, so obviously his brother could say a bit more than I'd thought. When we rang the door bell, Connor opened the door.

'Gran's in the kitchen. She's going to make us a cake.'

'Now, I'll not listen to any secrets,' called Connor's gran, 'but I would like to know whether it's chocolate or lemon you'll be wanting.'

Connor introduced Josh to his gran, and she said what a fine young man he was, and Josh seemed to grow another few centimetres.

Harry was late. He'd been to block B rather than block D, and then he'd waited ages for the lift until he twigged it wasn't working. He'd had to walk, as the au pair was out picking up special pancakes – 'blinis', Harry called them – that were supposed to go with the caviar.

'I've never been this way before, except in the Explorer,' he said with excitement. 'I mean, have you seen the graffiti on block B? It's a real work of art!'

When we were all settled, the doorbell went.

It was Adam. We never go to his house. Adam doesn't like us there for some reason, and I'd forgotten to ring him.

'Harry's mum was too busy to speak to me,' he said sourly, 'so I went round to Matthew's house and his dad said you were at Connor's gran's, and then I had to go round to Connor's flat to find out how to get to his gran's.'

He tried to look mean, but I could see he was really upset.

Connor's gran came into the living room.

'I thought I heard the bell. And you'll be the last lad they were waiting for, no doubt, so you tell me what it will be: chocolate cake or lemon cake?'

'Lemon,' said Adam, and he seemed to cheer up.

'So that's it,' I explained. 'It's nothing to do with us . . . just a dreadful poster of some oldies doing an ancient dance. No wonder they don't want to come.'

'Have to make a new poster,' said Josh.

'And get it to St Anne's,' Connor added.

'Isn't it a bit late?' worried Harry. 'The disco is meant to be next Friday.'

'What's it going to be a poster of?' said Adam.

We didn't have any ideas. We drew on bits of paper, tried out cartoon styles and fancy lettering, but none of it worked.

After a couple of hours, Connor's gran brought in the lemon cake.

'What glum faces,' she cried. 'Not my cake, I hope.'

'Yum!', 'Thanks!', 'Delicious!' we said.

It was the only good thing to come out of the afternoon.

'Will you not tell me your troubles?' said Connor's gran.

So we told her.

'Lovely boys that you are, just look at you. All you need is a nice picture of you all on your poster and every girl at St Anne's will be flocking.'

Connor's gran pointed to a side table covered with photos of her grandchildren. We got up and looked. There were photos of Connor and his big sisters at the seaside, and formal photos taken by the school photographer, but at the back was a photograph of Connor leaping in the air after the ball, socks fallen down, legs muddy. I recognised it all right. It was when a nasty throat bug had felled half the football team in October and Connor and Harry had made it off the substitutes' bench for the first and only time.

Behind Connor, Adam was running up at full tilt with a terrifying sneer on his face. And there was me! I was getting up off the ground, my kit all muddy and dirt on my face. And behind me I could see Harry strolling up, not a speck of dirt on him, apart from muddy boots. I'm sure Josh was hanging round on the edge with Luke, and there were lots more boys from our class in the background.

'Who took that?' I said.

'Dad,' said Connor.

'Lovely photo,' said Connor's gran. 'I like a boy dressed in his Sunday best, but this is a picture of real lads.'

'But surely the girls won't like that?' said Harry. 'I mean, we're all dirty and muddy.'

'I don't know,' I said. Connor isn't exactly a football star or a looker, and he was the biggest person in the photo. His dad must have waited ages to snap it. 'What do you think, Josh?'

Josh shrugged his shoulders.

'We've got nothing else,' said Connor, grinning at the photo as if it was a memento of an England trial.

'Yeah, we'll do it,' said Adam.

And because none of us had a better idea and we all felt guilty about having forgotten Adam, we agreed with him.

'I'll give it to my father's secretary,' said Harry. 'She can scan it in, blow it up and make colour prints.'

So we shoved Harry off as fast as we could to try and catch his father before the forty guests arrived.

Going home, it dawned on me that if the poster did work, and the girls did want to come to the disco, I still couldn't dance properly and I couldn't be seen dead in that vomit-coloured shirt. I'd just have to help Connor with the lights. No one would see me as long as I was careful not to walk out in front of any coloured beams, which might make me look like an orange or green Martian doing a galactic jig.

Amy was sitting at the kitchen table with Mum, painting Mum's fingernails with some beetroot-coloured goo out of a little bottle.

'I've been waiting for you, Matty,' she said.

'He's been out with his mates,' said Dad, coming in

122

from the living room. 'Where did you meet, then? Did you say Connor's place?'

'No, his gran's. She made us a lemon cake.'

'Did she now?' said Mum, who hasn't made a cake in years.

'And I expect you watched the football,' said Dad, grinning.

I know what he wants. He wants me to have lots of mates, 'nice lads' who watch football, so he knows he's got a popular son.

'I've got to go,' said Amy, putting the little brush back inside the bottle. She wobbled up on her purple shoes. 'But I came for a word with Matty first, in private.'

'Come on, tell us what it's about,' said Dad. 'You can't hide secrets from me.'

'It's a bit of advice for the disco, if you must know.'

Dad grinned. 'That's right, Amy. You tell him what's what. He's going to love that disco. There'll be no stopping him afterwards. I remember my first dance in the community hall . . .'

Amy dragged me off, her purple-painted talons digging into my arm.

'The black pants . . .' she whispered.

'Honest. I didn't need them,' I said.

'No . . . I've got them. When you weren't here, I came up to play with James so I could snoop round your room for them. James knew where they were . . . Good place, behind the computer.'

'Take them back, I don't want them.'

'It's OK. I found a plastic bucket under the kitchen sink, when Aunty Sue was out shopping. It's under James's bunk.'

Amy bent down, swaying dangerously on her purple shoes, and pulled out a red bucket. It was the bucket Mum used to wash the kitchen floor and it was full of dingy water and rags.

'It's working,' Amy said. 'I bought two pairs extra cheap in the market and put one in the wash, and now all our tea towels are black. Mum's hopping mad.'

'But what's in the bucket?'

'It's the second pair, of course. Mum wouldn't let me wear them, because she said they'd ruin the washing. Look, the colour's coming out nicely. Your shirt will look a lot better.'

'My shirt? Which shirt?'

'Your sicky shirt, stupid! The disgusting mustard-yellow shirt. We're dying it black. Black is great for discos. Black or white, they're the best colours.'

I stared into the bucket full of dark, murky water. It didn't look too good in there.

'I've got to dash to the new James Bond,' she announced. 'Leave it to soak overnight. Empty the bucket in the bathroom tomorrow and hang the shirt on the line. You'll look so much better. You can't go wrong with black.'

I thought of Josh in his black coat and suit with his black hair.

Black was interesting. A lot better than mustard yellow.

'Aren't you going to say thank you? I've sacrificed a pair of new lacy pants for you.'

'Thanks, Amy,' I said, and I meant it. My huge weight of worries had grown a little lighter. 'Come round on Monday. I'll keep you some biscuits and you can see how the shirt has turned out.'

Eighteen

That evening it pelted with rain. Dad had planned to take us all to the cinema, but when Mum opened the door and saw the rain gushing out of the drain-pipe, overflowing from the blocked drain and racing down the front path, she said, 'How many times have I told you, Simon, that the drain is blocked with leaves?'

Dad stared at the drain in mock surprise.

'Since when is cleaning the leaves out of the drain a male job. I thought our new-style arrangement was non-sexist.'

Mum was stumped.

'Well . . . we're not going out in this downpour,' she declared. 'The forecast is storms all night. We'll be better off with a video at home.'

So Dad went to the video shop with orders from Mum to get two pizzas as well.

'Dad, can we have some crisps?' I said. 'Some of those new tandoori poppadom crisps, and some paprika and shrimp crunchies, and some chive and cheese curls?'

'If you want crisps,' said Dad, 'you can get the red bucket out and clean the leaves from the drain.'

I didn't dare protest in case someone else went looking for the bucket, so I got soaked, standing out in the rain, raking the dead leaves out of the drain. I had to stuff them, all wet and slimy, into an empty cereal box I found in the dustbin. Still, it did the job. The rain went nicely down the drain, gurgling away. I felt quite pleased with myself.

'Well done,' said Mum.

Dad came back with a mixed multipack of crisps. The mixed selections always have the most boring crisps, but Mum said she didn't mind the plain, so I grabbed the cheese and onion.

The pizzas weren't bad either.

The next morning, Sunday, it was still raining. The raindrops spattered on the windows and gave them the wash Dad never got round to doing. Mum was curled up on the sofa with a coffee and a magazine. James was sitting on the floor drawing and Dad was working on his plans for the attic extension for my new bedroom.

I went up to my room and got out my geography book. Last test!

I read it all through. I was surprised how much I remembered. I think I like geography. I was feeling quite confident about a test, for a change.

Then I put on Kiss FM and practised my dancing in front of the mirror. I couldn't feel the beat any better than before, but I came up with a brilliant wheeze. If I kept my feet in the same place, never moving them, I could move my hips and arms and bend my knees. It was sort of swaying around to the music.

I knew it didn't look great, but it didn't look so ridiculous either. Not that I was going to need it anyway, if I stayed behind the lights with Connor.

Last of all I tiptoed into the bathroom with the red bucket, squeezed out my yucky shirt and . . . it was a dirty grey. Much better than dirty yellow.

I squeezed the pants out – they were less black than they had been – and stuffed them back down behind the computer. I couldn't hang the shirt outside, because of the rain, so I crept downstairs and bunged it in the drier in the kitchen. I reckoned that if it was going to shrink it would have done so already with all the soaking.

'You did a thorough job with the leaves last night,' said Dad, coming into the kitchen and getting a beer out of the fridge. 'Good lad. Don't leave the bucket sitting on the floor for one of us to fall over. Put it back under the sink. That's one thing you should learn, Matthew, always finish a job.'

It was on the tip of my tongue to mention the attic,

but somehow I felt it would shatter the rare mood of peace in the house.

Monday it was still raining.

We had the geography test first thing and I quite enjoyed it. I don't think I got too much wrong.

'Where's Harry?' I said to Josh at break, as we broke into a packet of cucumber and sour cream tasties.

'He's gone to London,' said Adam, as he pulled back the ring of his can and sprayed my clean, white shirt with foam. 'He's got an appointment.'

'But he's meant to be photocopying our poster,' I said.

'Perhaps he's having it done in London,' Josh said.

'He's not,' said Adam. 'Because he rang me and he was really mad that he was going.'

'Who made him go?'

'His mum.'

We crunched and swallowed.

'Clothes,' said Josh. 'She'll have taken him shopping for the disco.'

So that was it! Harry isn't bad-looking anyway, and he always has smart gear, so if he'd gone to London to buy up all the latest stuff, the girls would mob him. I'd certainly be staying behind the lights in my dirty grey shirt.

'It's not fair,' I said.

The others nodded. Being stinking rich without us in on it is criminal.

★

We didn't do much work the rest of the day. No one was in the mood now the tests were over and I reckon the staff were too busy marking them. I had this wild, exhilarating sense of relief that they were all over. I couldn't do anything more. My fate was decided. Now I was going to enjoy myself, because one thing was for sure: the axe would fall soon enough.

'Coming to Mr Patel's?' I said to Josh at the end of school.

'Might do,' he said, pulling on his jacket.

We passed a new notice in the hall saying that, because of exceptional rain, the pitches were flooding and in no state for football the next day. Instead we were going to have a cross–country run.

'Great!' I said.

Cross–country runs mean you can hide behind bushes with a can and a bag of crisps, chatting to your mates.

'It's the track round the golf course,' said Josh, who hates running. 'I think I'll have a sore throat.'

'It would never work with my mum,' I said. 'Come on, we can get some supplies from Mr Patel. I've still got some pocket money left.'

Josh had a few coins, so we pooled our cash.

'I've been waiting for you two to come in,' said Mr Patel. 'Look at these. Now there's something extra-ordinary.'

He held up two gold and blue striped crisp bags.

'What are they?' I said, interested.

'Hummus and radish flavour.'

'What on earth will that taste like?'

'You'll have to find out. They're new, launched only yesterday.'

So we stocked up on the stripy crisps – and a couple of packets of smoky bacon to be on the safe side – some cans of cola and two KitKats. It was going to be a great run the next day.

Despite the pelting rain and my sodden jacket, I was feeling really cheerful when I got home. I'd get Kiss FM on in my room and have a good work-out of my new dance routine. No revising tonight!

Mum was home. She made me a cup of tea and found me some biscuits. That was a bit odd, as I usually had to do it myself. Then she sat down at the kitchen table, elbows on the table, chin in her hands, staring at me as I ate. It was unnerving.

James came in and whined for a biscuit. Mum gave him one and shooed him back into the living room to watch television.

Then I saw the letter lying on the table. It had St David's School for Boys across the top. My heart sank. The tests must have been disastrous. Perhaps I was being suspended. But hold on . . . I'd only finished the geography test that day. I couldn't be suspended for doing badly in one or two subjects, could I?

'Matthew, are you happy?'

I looked up in surprise. Strange question. Since

when had anyone been concerned about happiness in our house? It's all about working hard, passing exams and getting good jobs in our place.

'I'm relieved the tests are over.'

'I mean, if you're not happy, if there's anything you're worried about . . .'

'I'm always worried, Mum. So are you and Dad.'

'What I wanted to say is that we're here if you ever want to speak to us. We'll always have the time to listen . . .'

I munched my biscuit. Some joke. Nobody had time to listen to anybody in our family.

'OK,' I said, pushing my chair back and leaving my dirty mug on the table.

I waited for Mum to tell me not to be so lazy and wash up my mug, but she didn't.

'And if there are some things you find it difficult to talk to us about, like growing up, working out who you are, about becoming a man, the school says they have this teacher, Miss Frankel, who is a trained counsellor . . .'

Miss Frankel . . . Who on earth was she? Then I remembered that she was a part-time art teacher who wore brilliantly coloured clothes. I don't have much to do with her, as I'm lousy at art.

'Maybe it would be a good idea to have a little talk with her, Matthew.'

About what? Did everybody think I was such a dud case that I was going nutty? Perhaps I was too stupid to see it. And what was all this about growing into a man?

I thought that was one of the last things I had to worry about. Didn't it just happen?

No, I had enough on my mind without having to complicate it with Miss Frankel.

'No, Mum, I'm fine,' I said, and escaped upstairs to my room.

It was quite a relief to get Kiss FM on and try out my sway dance. I was getting to really like Kiss FM. The thumping music relaxed me and shut me off from all the madness downstairs.

Nineteen

We were all relieved to see Harry back in the cloakroom as we took off our jackets at school the next day. Adam pushed in behind him, carrying a long cardboard tube.

'I'll hide it under your cross-country kit,' he whispered to Harry.

'It's the poster!' I said. 'Come on, let's see it.'

'No,' said Adam self-importantly. 'We don't want it damaged.'

Harry nodded.

'Go on, Harry, let me look. I'll be ever so careful.'

Harry shook his head.

'You heard,' said Adam. 'We said no.'

'Harry can speak for himself,' said Connor, who was obviously dying to see himself as the football star.

Harry shook his head again.

'Can't you talk?' said Josh.

Harry nodded. We stared.

'Harry doesn't want to answer any questions,' said Adam.

'He's not gone dumb, has he?' I asked. 'I know he's dimwitted . . .'

'A right thicko . . .' baited Josh.

'A stupid . . . stupid . . .' Connor struggled to find an insult. 'Oh, just tell us, Harry. What's the matter?'

Harry turned away, but I grabbed his arm.

'We're your mates,' I said.

'Oh, all right. I'll have to talk sometime.'

It was amazing! Harry's mouth glittered with silver wires and tiny bands. Every tooth was imprisoned in shining wire contraptions.

'Did they do that to you in London?' I gasped.

'My mother says I've got to grow up with perfect teeth,' spluttered Harry. 'Yesterday I had to go to this dentist in Harley Street. But at least I got the poster blown up while I was in London.'

We wiped the spray from Harry's mouth off our sweatshirts.

So that was it in a nutshell. There are considerable disadvantages to being seriously rich, but on the other hand you can get a poster blown up in London.

'Let me look,' said Connor. He peered up into Harry's mouth. 'That's a miracle of miniature engineering. Maybe I should think of being a dental engineer instead.'

'But the disco . . .' Harry moaned.

And we saw his point. It might be a miracle of engineering, but it wasn't a great selling point with the girls.

'They won't notice, Harry,' I said, because I was afraid he'd drop out of helping. 'With your smart clothes, no one's going to look at your teeth.'

'Don't talk,' said Josh helpfully.

'I think it looks a great bit of wiring,' said Connor.

I dug him in the ribs to shut him up, but I think we were all feeling a little more cheerful. In my dirty grey shirt, I reckoned I'd got as much chance of impressing any girls as Harry in the disco stakes.

After lunch we changed into our cross-country kit. Josh and I stuffed the cans, crisps and KitKats up under our sports shirts. Harry stuck the cardboard tube down the back of his shirt, tucked into his shorts elastic. Connor had remembered a box of drawing pins. Adam kept lookout while we changed and stayed as cover at the back when we set off.

We ran out of the school gates, with Mr Temple, the football coach, hurrying us on.

'Get a move on, lads,' he yelled. 'If you're flagging now, what will you be like after six kilometres?'

'Six kilometres,' Harry groaned. 'I've never even walked that far in my life.'

We ran in a bunch at the front, down the road and onto the track beside the golf course. After ten minutes we were already puffing and groaning.

136

'That big holly bush ... under the trees ... further on, on the right,' I gasped. 'Stop there.'

We allowed a group of enthusiasts to overtake us and then we slipped behind the bushes.

'If I had my mobile,' said Harry's flashing mouth, 'I'd get the au pair to come and collect us in the Explorer.'

We shared the crisps and KitKats. Adam produced a Mars Bar, Connor a cheese sandwich his gran had made him the day before and Harry a can of exotic nuts he'd nicked from his parents' buffet supper. He pulled back the little tab and shared them round. They were green, but Harry said they weren't mouldy and wouldn't give us a tummy upset.

'Stop spitting over them, Harry,' said Connor. 'You'll contaminate the nuts.'

'I can't help it, with this brace,' Harry moaned. 'But don't worry about me. I won't have anything. The crisps keep getting stuck in these wires.'

Talk about torture!

'We'd better get moving,' I said, peering round the prickly holly bush. 'We're last now, so we'll be able to slip into St Anne's without anyone seeing.'

'But if we're too late back,' said Connor, 'they'll come looking for us.'

We were exhausted by the time we staggered up to St Anne's. Our hair was plastered down in wet rat's-tails. Our trainers were soggy and heavy with mud, and there were brown splashes all the way up our legs. Even the backs of our shirts and shorts were spattered where we must have kicked up the mud as we ran.

I was shattered. It wasn't six kilometres, surely. It had to be a marathon. We pushed through a hole in the hedge onto the road beside the girls' school.

It was deadly quiet. School wasn't over yet and the girls must have been stuck in lessons.

'Where are we going to put the poster?' said Adam.

We looked around. The railings were no good, because we couldn't get the pins into the metal.

'We can pin it to the school sign,' said Connor.

Inside the gate stood a tall wooden sign:

St Anne's School for Girls
Head teacher: Mrs Eleanor Hinton–Gore, BA, MA, Dip. Ed.
Caretaker: Mr Roy Scutts

Josh rattled the gate. It was locked.

'Can't get in,' he said.

'Course we can,' said Adam. 'I'll do it.'

Adam limbered up and was over in seconds. I think he's had plenty of practice climbing tall gates.

'Pass me through the cardboard tube,' he said as he dropped down on the other side.

Harry pulled the long tube out from under the back of his shirt and passed it through the railings. Adam unfurled the poster.

'Look at that,' I said. 'It's brilliant.'

The photograph had been blown up into a giant poster. It was so clear you could see every speck of mud and dirt – except on Harry, whose kit looked as if it had been through a washing powder ad on telly. Connor seemed halfway to heaven, his feet off the ground, his wiry red hair flaming. Adam towered murderously. And there was me, struggling up off the ground, looking . . . well, muddy. Josh was chatting to Luke, and behind them were half the rest of the class shouting or grinning.

At the bottom in big gold letters was:

St David's Year Seven Xmas disco!
The place to be seen . . . Do you dare?
Friday, 16 December, 7 pm
A limited number of tickets available
from Mr Grinston at St David's

We stared in amazement. It was really professional.

'The man in the poster shop suggested the first two lines,' said Harry, looking worried at our blank faces. 'And my mother suggested the ticket line, because she said all the best parties have to be exclusive, not too many tickets.'

'All right on the sports pages,' said Josh at last.

'What do you mean? Won't the girls like it?' I said, suddenly worried.

'Girls don't like dirt and mud,' said Josh, who must know, because his brothers have girlfriends.

'That's right,' said Connor. 'My sisters spend hours in the bathroom and they don't even like football.'

Too late. Adam had pinned the poster to the board and was scrambling back over the gate.

'Duck!' I whispered. 'Some girls are looking out of that classroom window.'

'Isn't that the caretaker coming over?' said Harry, panic in his voice.

The caretaker plodded up, ignored us as if we were the scum of the earth, and unlocked the gates. At the same moment a stream of girls poured from the front door into the playground, carrying their school bags. We couldn't risk being recognised by Stephanie and Zoe.

'Duck behind the cars,' Adam ordered.

The road was filling up with cars parking beside the pavement. I looked at my watch. Three-thirty already!

We ducked down behind a white estate car, just in time. We could hear the girls giggling on the other side of the fence.

'Come and look at this.'

'Football poster . . . Ooh! They're yucky and muddy.'

'Did you see those boys at the gates? They were absolutely filthy. Did you see them running away?'

'What's it about? . . . A disco, a football disco!'

So it was obvious they'd missed the point. They'd never come if they thought they had to wear football kit.

'Do you mind?' said a voice above me. 'I've just been

to the car wash and I don't want muddy marks on my clean car.'

We moved back and a mother, her face wrinkled in a frown, poked her head out of the window. Her white car was covered in muddy handprints, like the pictures James used to make in nursery school.

Then all the waiting mothers wound down their windows. We hadn't noticed them sitting there to keep out of the rain.

'What exactly are you lot up to?' said another mother, shaking her head in disapproval. 'Did I see . . .'

'Scram!' said Adam.

So we ran.

Twenty

We pelted out into the main road, laughing and falling over.

'We've done it,' I shouted.

'You should have seen that mother's face,' giggled Harry.

'Leg it,' yelled Adam. 'If the St Anne's lot ring St David's we should be in the playground, mingling with the other boys. That way they can't spot us.'

And we ran flat out, because Adam knows about these things.

As we puffed up to the St David's gates, Connor grabbed my arm. 'Look, there's your dad.'

I turned. It was Dad all right, parked on the other side of the road in our old Ford. My heart sank. I had been planning to buy another packet of hummus and radish crisps from Mr Patel and I'd been looking forward to walking home with Josh and Connor to discuss the day's events.

Dad never came to fetch me. Mum didn't even come any longer.

Dad wound down his window. 'Don't bother to change, Matthew. Just fetch your school clothes and come straight out.'

I was feeling really let down as I clambered into the car. I chucked my school clothes and bag on the back seat. Dad turned and gave me an odd smile, the sort he gives people he's nervous with. He was gripping the steering wheel with white knuckles.

'All in, then, are we?' he said heartily, as our ageing Ford chugged away from St David's.

Dad talked about the cross-country run and whether I'd had any test results yet.

'We could have given Josh a lift,' I said.

'Ah, Josh, yes, that brings me to ... I mean ... Well, dammit Matthew, have you been helping yourself to your mother's lipstick? You know she doesn't like you and James rummaging in our bedroom.'

'I certainly haven't taken her lipstick,' I said indignantly.

Dad stared intently out of the front window and then sucked in a deep breath.

'Man to man, Matthew, I have to tell you that the school caretaker's wife saw you using her back window to – her words not mine – "apply a great smudge of lipstick" to your mouth.'

'How did she know it was me?'

'So you admit it! She recognised you, because she said you were the nice boy in the playground who helped her pick up her scattered potatoes when her bag broke last week as she was carrying in her shopping.'

'Well, it wasn't Mum's lipstick,' I said sulkily.

Dad sat silent, as if thinking carefully what to say.

'But that's not the point, Matthew. Why do you want to wear lipstick, and why do you have to put it on hiding in little back alleys?'

'I had to be a woman,' I said. 'That's why I wore it.'

It was obvious, wasn't it?

Dad stared straight ahead. When he spoke his voice came out all strangled. 'Why do you want to be a girl, Matthew?'

'Actually, I wasn't being a girl. Connor was the girl.'

'Does his mother know about this?' whispered Dad.

'No, but his gran does.'

Dad swallowed and nodded.

'If you weren't pretending to be a girl, what did you want the lipstick for?'

'I was being a mum. I didn't want to be a mother, but Josh said I had to be.'

'Josh – he's your new friend, wears all those ridiculous clothes, right?'

'They're not ridiculous. I think he borrows them off his big brothers and they're supposed to be really cool.'

'But why, Matthew? Mum and I want to help and understand. It's all come as rather a shock. We thought you were such an . . . ordinary boy. Can you tell us?'

'Look, Dad, I can't tell you yet. It's confidential. So don't ask.'

When we got home, I shook Dad off by disappearing into my bedroom. I turned Kiss FM on loud. My shirt was quite dry now. Dirty grey is definitely better than dirty mustard.

I heard Mum come in. She and Dad sat for ages in the kitchen with the door shut. Then the angry rumbles started. I turned off the radio and opened my door when the telephone rang.

Dad beat me to the phone in the hall, shouting, 'If you weren't so obsessed with your job . . .'

'If you were a better father and shouldered your share of caring . . .' came Mum's furious voice.

Their nagging was getting worse. I didn't like it.

'Sue,' called Dad, 'it's for you – Julie.'

Julie is Zoe's mum.

Twenty-one

The next day, when I came back from school, they were both at home. That was odd, because usually when one is at home the other is at work, and it was Dad's day to stay late at work. I didn't even have to see the car to know Dad was home. You could hear the shouting several doors away.

I had my test results.

I'd been practising what I'd say all afternoon, but no one was going to hear me above that din.

I pushed open the back door. Mum was standing by the sink, waving the dish mop and yelling, 'But, Simon, can't I get it into your head, I DON'T WANT TO MOVE. I've got a good job at last, promotion coming up. NO . . . I'm simply not going to. How can you be so thoughtless and mean?'

Dad was sitting at the table, his head in his hands. His face was crumpled and his shoulders sagged.

'I've been telling you and telling you,' he tried desperately, 'but you won't listen, Sue. It's not me being unreasonable. The company is moving, amalgamating with the branch in Barchester. It's a job in Barchester or no job at all.'

Mum gulped in a furious breath and turned to face him.

'You're going on your own to Barchester. I'm not coming, giving up my job. The years I've spent looking after this family. It's my turn now. My one chance to have a decent career . . .'

'I know all that, Sue,' said Dad, his voice tight with anger. 'But this is about money. How am I going to support the family without a job?'

'The children will stay with me,' said Mum. 'You can come home at the weekend.'

'That's nearly 500 kilometres, round trip! You must be mad if you think I'm going to spend all my well-earned weekend in the car, just to get here to be told to make the bed or empty the washing machine. And it'll cost a fortune in petrol.'

'Dad, I've got my test results.'

'Are you implying we'd be better off separated?' yelled Mum.

'Mum, I've got an A in maths and geography.'

I waved my results at her. She was like someone mad. She stared at them but she didn't take them in.

'*And* an A in French.'

I felt bad about the A in French. That was Harry's A. I hadn't intended to tell them, but I reckoned this was a desperate situation.

'I never mentioned separation,' groaned Dad. 'Why do you always jump to wild conclusions, Sue? All you need is to be calm and rational about this. I think you'll be surprised by the job situation up in Barchester. You'll have no difficulty—'

'I am not giving up my job, Simon. Never! And what about Matthew, settled in now at St David's? Haven't you any consideration for your own son?'

'Dad, I got a B in general science and in history.'

Dad stared at me as blindly as Mum. It was like their row was cutting them off in a glass bubble.

'*My* son?' He pointed. '*Your* son, you mean. If you hadn't gone dashing back to work full-time, would he have the problems he has now?'

'How dare you, Simon!'

'I got a C in technology,' I muttered.

It wasn't fair. I couldn't help being hopeless at English and technology. Why was it such a problem?

'And a D in English,' I whispered.

I guess that was a problem now.

Dad was staring at me strangely.

'It's OK, Dad. I'm going to get some extra help with my English,' I tried to explain.

'Oh, Matthew,' said Dad dramatically, all sort of sad and angry the way parents are on telly. 'How can I leave

148

you with your mother now? You'll have to come with me.'

'Hold on,' I said. 'I'm staying at St David's. We're hoping to get the disco going for Friday, and I've got a new shirt to wear, so I can't make Barchester at the moment.'

'Well, you're not wearing these,' said Dad, as he fished something out of his pocket. He held up Amy's faded black lacy pants. 'I found them stuffed down behind the computer when I unplugged the printer this afternoon. James says they are yours.'

Mum's hand shot up to her face.

She swayed and then her voice came in a squeak: 'The lipstick. Zoe saw him in St Anne's with lipstick, women's clothes. Don't be angry with him, Simon. He needs help, some counselling. We've got him an appointment.'

'A boy of mine . . .' Dad muttered darkly.

Thank heavens the door opened and in tottered Amy. She stared at Mum and Dad.

'Aunty Sue, I could hear you down the street. My mum and dad at least have their rows with a bit of decent quiet. Oh, thanks, Uncle Simon. Those are mine.' Amy stretched out her hand and took the lacy black pants. 'I was just coming to ask Matty to give them back. Mum says they probably won't run in the wash now they've had a good soaking.'

Suddenly I understood. It was all clear.

I started to laugh. It rumbled up from deep inside and burst out like a volcano erupting.

Me . . . a girl! Mum should have been delighted. She's always saying she wished she had a daughter. And I was relieved, so relieved. I'd survived the tests . . . just about. I'd been dreading telling them my results, facing the usual interrogation, and they hadn't even noticed. It was my lucky day!

I laughed till I spluttered and coughed, so that Amy ended up thumping me on the back.

'Matthew, you're making a worse din than Uncle Simon and Aunty Sue.'

'Counselling,' I giggled. 'Will that get me out of extra English?' and I roared at my own joke.

Mum and Dad were silently watching me and then they stared at each other. They hadn't a clue what was happening.

So I told them about the sicky yellow shirt. How I'd soaked it black, or rather dirty grey. And I only told them about the trip to St Anne's once they'd promised not to be cross with me.

Mum looked disapproving, but a grin spread across Dad's face.

'That's a good one,' said Dad.

'Simon!' said Mum.

'Cancel that appointment with the counsellor at the surgery,' said Dad. 'He won't be needing it now.'

'Why me?' said Mum indignantly. 'You can cancel it.'

And I could see they were just about to start up again.

'Don't cancel it,' I said. 'You and Mum go.'

'Counselling,' spluttered Dad. 'For me?'

'I'm much too busy,' said Mum quickly. 'And there's no need. We can sort our own problems out . . .'

'But you can't,' I insisted. 'You and Dad are always yelling at each other, and it's getting worse and worse.'

They glared at me as if I was making it all up.

'How will I ever be able to do any homework in this house, revise for exams to get to college, to get a good job, with the nag, nag, nagging that goes on here?'

'Well . . .' said Dad.

'Hm . . .' said Mum.

And I think that, for the first time, they were really listening.

Twenty-two

Mr Grinston looked like some demented owl when all the year assembled in the hall for our last meeting of term. His grizzly curls shook round his startled face and his eyes were wide and staring.

He rushed through all the usual notices about too much litter in the classrooms and not stopping work just because the tests were over. Usually he loves the sound of his own voice and going on about things. But today . . .

'And finally – and this is very short notice – the Christmas disco will be taking place tomorrow, after all.'

He paused and gazed round us triumphantly.

'The ticket applications over the last twenty-four hours have been quite remarkable. The girls of St Anne's have obviously not learned about the benefits of planning and organisation in their personal lives, but have left it, most inconsiderately, until the last moment.'

Around us whistling and cheers broke out. I glanced at Josh, Connor, Harry and Adam sitting alongside me. We grinned.

Done it!

And I'd learned something: girls don't mind muddy boys, so they must like football more than they let on.

Then old Grinston went on and on about the arrangements. Connor was responsible with his dad for lighting, Harry was in charge of decorating and Luke was helping put tickets into envelopes with each girl's name on. Those of us who were left had to volunteer and write our names on a huge sheet of paper marked ACTION PLAN.

The DECORATING and LIGHTING slots had already been filled by Harry and Connor, but underneath LIGHTING: Connor O'Brien, I squeezed in in tiny writing Matthew Evans.

Nobody would notice me there. I'd switch the lights on and off for Connor, because suddenly I wasn't too confident about my sway dancing. What if it looked ridiculous? What if someone laughed at me?

The rest of the day was nothing like a normal school day. The tests over, we didn't do a stroke of work, but worked flat out to get the gym ready for the disco. Harry decided we should decorate it with a football theme, like the poster, so we borrowed football flags and scarves and posters and hung them on the wall bars and ladders. Then we draped silver and gold tinsel on top.

Connor's dad came in to help Connor set up the lighting. I don't know why he wasn't at work. He was a bit wheezy, so Connor kept insisting he rest on a chair while giving instructions.

'Connor,' I said, 'you know I'm meant to be your assistant . . .'

Me! Connor's assistant. How low had I sunk?

Connor stared at me, puzzled. 'I was meaning to say about that, Matthew. You don't know anything about lighting. Thanks, but St Anne's are providing someone to help work the lights. Someone who knows what they're doing.'

What was I going to do? Where could I disappear? I was more worried, more panic-stricken than I'd ever been in my life.

Mum had said she and Dad would always be there if I wanted to talk. But they weren't. They were away at this counsellor's place. Mum left ready-made meals for me and James to put in the microwave. Then when Mum and Dad came back they ate by themselves and talked and talked. I opened the door into the kitchen but they shut up immediately, and said, 'What do you want, Matthew?'

'Nothing,' I said, and crept upstairs to my room and tried a pathetic sway or two in front of the mirror.

I tried on my shirt. It was a bit tight and not as black as I'd hoped, and I wished my hair stood up like Josh's. I opened the tin of bee's wax I'd found in the cleaning cupboard and combed a little through my hair. It had this powerful, furniture sort of smell and my hair stood up like it was cemented. It didn't have that shiny, deep black colour of Josh's, more a scuffed-brown shoe colour.

I discovered my best trousers still in the dirty-washing basket under a pile of smelly clothes.

'Mum!' I broke into the intense discussion in the kitchen.

'What do you want, Matthew?'

'My trousers haven't been washed. I need them for the disco tomorrow.'

'Disco?' Mum ran her hand through her untidy hair. 'Oh, the disco. Half a cup of soap powder, right compartment, cotton, 40°.'

So, even if I hadn't learned how to dance, I'd learned how to wash trousers.

It's Friday evening. I'm ready. Trousers clean, but crumpled (I haven't learned how to iron yet and Mum and Dad are out again). Grey-black T-shirt. Josh is calling round. We're going together.

The doorbell rings.

Josh looks terrific, all in black – long black coat, black hair combed up, black shades and it's dark outside. I ask you . . .

I run my fingers through my hair, trying to get it to stand up.

'Don't do that,' says Josh. 'It looks a mess.'

155

He's absolutely right. I'm a mess. My heart is pounding and even as we saunter down the cold street my hands are hot and sweaty. But at least I've got Josh. I can hide behind him and watch how he dances. He knows about these things.

Girls are giggling and laughing as they stream across the playground. Tall girls, short girls, thin girls, cuddly girls – and they all look happy.

Keep calm, I tell myself, don't panic.

'Hi, Matthew!' It's Zoe in a pretty silvery jacket. 'Want to borrow my lipstick?'

I cringe. Nowhere to hide.

'Yeah!' I say, in a voice that doesn't sound like me at all, 'but only if it's Raging Red. I'm not wearing any of that cheap pink stuff.'

The girls with Zoe laugh, and Zoe says, 'You're a one, Matthew.'

Did I really say that? I did! And the girls laughed.

Josh stops at the door to the gym. It's dim in there, with coloured lights flashing on and off and loud music pouring out.

'Come on, Josh.'

'Nah. I'm staying at the door. Helping Luke with the tickets.'

'Why?'

'Got to practise my bodyguarding skills. Mustn't let anyone in who shouldn't be here.'

Josh stands at the door in his shades. I bet he can't even see the tickets, but he looks good.

156

I'm alone.

I go in and stand by the wall. Harry sidles up. I recognise him by his flashing mouth. We talk about football and watch the girls dancing in the middle out of the corner of our eyes.

Then this huge, tall girl comes up. It's Amanda! She's seen me. She's coming to say 'Hi'.

'Hi,' she says to Harry.

He smiles with his mouth tight shut. It looks as if he's grimacing.

'I came to say "Snap!"' she says, and a spray of spit lands on Harry.

And then I see that her mouth is flashing silver too.

Harry grins. 'When did you get yours?' he says as he sprays Amanda back.

'My top canines are crossing my premolars, so I've got to wear this for a year,' says Amanda, sticking her fingers in her mouth.

'I've got a faulty bite,' explains Harry. 'Receding lower incisors.'

'Fancy dancing?' says Amanda.

And that's the last I see of Harry. Some mate! And Amanda didn't even notice me . . .

I can see Adam, leaping around on the dance floor like a mad grasshopper. He's showing off. Some girls are laughing, but he doesn't seem to mind.

I wouldn't be seen dead . . .

Got to find Connor.

Poor Connor, he's stuck behind a hot spotlight. His

face is shiny with sweat. And you'll never guess what . . .
He's wearing a sicky mustard-coloured T-shirt with a
brown trim. I bet I know who sold him that.

I pull down my grey-black shirt . . . It might be on
the tight side, but at least it's no longer vomit-coloured.
The strange thing is, the dirty mustard T-shirt looks
quite good on Connor with his red hair and freckles. It
doesn't look yucky at all.

'Want some help?' I say.

'No thanks, Matthew. Dad and me and Francesca
have got it all under control. You'd mess it up.'

And there's this girl with dark curly hair, in a pink
shiny dress, saying, 'I think we should try the orange,
Connor. I'll check the cable.'

I wander off and try to stand near a group of girls.
They're all so tall, bigger than me, and they chatter non-
stop. I know they know that I'm there, because I can see
them looking sideways at me. But I can't barge in.
They're like a tight rugby scrum.

Lots of people are dancing now. I'm feeling silly,
walking up and down on my own. I try to hide behind
a light, but I trip over its legs. I'm falling on the dance
floor, so I pretend to be dancing. Sort of swaying and
bobbing my knees.

'Ow!' says a voice behind. 'That's my foot.'

'Sorry,' I say.

'It's OK,' says the girl.

She's small, with a lopsided smile and long fair hair
held back with a sparkly pin. And she starts dancing

opposite me and she doesn't seem to notice my swaying sort of dance, or if she does she doesn't mind.

The music stops and then it starts again, and we dance again and again.

'I'm hot,' she says.

'Do you want a drink?'

So I get her a cola and one for myself.

'Were you one of the boys outside St Anne's?' she says.

Does she mean the open day or when we put the poster up? Do I admit it?

'I helped put the poster up.'

'I thought I recognised you. I was looking out of the window in our French lesson.'

She's called Toni, short for Antonia, and she lives on the other side of town, which is why she didn't go to my junior school.

'What's St David's like?'

'OK.'

'What do you get up to out of school?'

'Not much.'

She's staring away from me, across the gym. I'm boring her.

'I hang around with my mates,' I say quickly, 'and . . . and I do karate.' But she's walking away. It's not surprising really. I'm too ordinary.

Now she's waving, beckoning me. I start off in a run and slow down quickly. I don't want to look stupid.

'Meet my best friend, Tammy,' she says, and she puts

her arm round this skinny tall girl dressed in sparkly white. 'And this is Shazia and Kelly and Momtaz.'

There's a whole crowd of girls and they're chatting and laughing and glittering in every colour you can think of.

'We saw you.'

'Our teacher made us pull down the blinds.'

'We gave up on our lesson.'

'Yes . . . well . . .'

Harry is coming over with Amanda. He'll help.

'You lot look good enough to put on the Christmas tree,' splutters Harry. 'You'd make better decorations than those glass balls.'

The girls smile and giggle some more. How does Harry do it? Where did he learn it?

'I love this,' says Toni as some new music starts over the sound system.

I know it. I've heard it lots of times on the radio. All the girls start dancing around in a big group. Somebody slaps me on the arm.

'Come on!' says Toni, and she drags me into the group.

Harry is dancing and so is Amanda. No one notices my dancing, as they only seem to concentrate on their own. I twist my hips, bend my knees and wave my arms above my head. It's great! I'm jogging around in and out of the girls and back to Toni, because I'm keen on Toni. Adam joins us and he's still leaping like some demented grasshopper.

'Go on!' we shout at Adam and he leaps higher . . .

and slips and falls. We all laugh and the girls pull him up, which he doesn't mind at all.

It's great . . . it's the best disco ever, not that I've been to one before, but I'm sure it is. So I go on dancing until, slap! shove! Someone is pushing and digging into my back and it hurts.

'Get off!' I yell.

I turn and there's this man I've never seen before, in a hairy tweed jacket with a grizzled goatee beard. He's staring at me, blinking in the flashing lights. A heavy fist grips my arm. 'Where's Antonia? They said she was over here,' he shouts.

Toni's hiding behind me.

'Antonia, I said you should be outside the door at nine o'clock. I'll not have you staying out late at your age. No . . . I can see a lot of kids are still dancing, but you're coming home, NOW! I've waited long enough outside in the cold. I've been forced to come in and look for you, and you know what we agreed . . .'

I say, 'Goodbye,' and 'See you around.' And I feel like telling her I know what parents are like too, but I can't with her dad standing there.

She's gone but I'm walking on air. Why does term have to end today? If it was school on Monday I could dash round to St Anne's after lessons and pretend to bump into her as she came out. Now I'll have to wait until January. It's the first time in my life I can't wait for Christmas to be over.

The lights go all dark and there's this smoochy last

161

dance. What a joke! A lot of the girls are taller than us, but they try to dance cheek to cheek with the boys. Their bums stick out as they bend to be shorter, and they keep bumping into each other.

I walk out. Josh is still wearing his shades on the door. There's a little group of girls shivering in the cold and chatting to him. He looks happy enough, but it's a shame I never saw him dance.

Harry dashes past with Amanda. Amanda's dad has driven up in the same silver Peugeot they had when we were at school together. Harry is writing something on the back of a disco ticket, until Amanda's dad blasts on the horn and she runs clutching the ticket in her hand.

And, no! There's Dad, leaning out of the car window, grinning all over his face . . .

Twenty-three

'Groovy time?' says Dad, on the way home.

'OK,' I say.

'And the girls,' he says anxiously. 'Pretty girls?'

'OK,' I say.

'Now, tell us all about it,' says Mum when I get into the kitchen.

'Nah, I'm tired,' I say.

Mum looks disappointed and I feel mean, but the disco . . . and Toni . . . it's my secret. I don't want to share it.

As I close my bedroom door, I hear Mum saying, 'Do you think the moody teens are striking?'

I don't wait to listen to Dad's reply, because, frankly it doesn't interest me.

★

But it didn't all end there. A lot of things came out of that disco.

Connor has a Saturday job in the electrical shop in town owned by Francesca's father. And that's good news, because I didn't know Connor's father was off work, sick with heart disease. I sometimes pop in for a chat when I can't think what else to do on a Saturday, or when I'm hanging around, hoping to bump into Toni out shopping with her mum. Connor's usually there, stacking light bulbs with Francesca.

Harry still has his brace. He's planning a party for when it comes off and he's going to invite Amanda and he says he'll invite Francesca and Toni if we want. So I'm not against spending a fortune on perfect teeth, so long as I'm invited.

And Harry's dad has bought a villa in Spain, which has solved the problem of being put in the top set for French after my A test result. I wouldn't have understood a word. Now I've changed to Spanish, and so have Adam and Josh and Luke and Kevin, as we're mates. I'm still trying to persuade Connor that Spain is not too hot and he won't get burnt.

Josh is still Josh, dressed in black, with some new shades. There's no one else in our year so cool, but here's a strange thing – I've never yet seen him dance.

My news is that I'm always starving and hungry. I need a lot more than crisps now. I'm growing . . . fast. Mum says I'll soon be taller than most of the girls.

Girls grow first, she says, but I'll soon catch up and will probably be bigger and stronger.

The biggest news of all is Mum and Dad. Dad hasn't gone to Barchester after all. He admitted to this counsellor that he'd hated his job for years, while Mum was mad on her job and doing brilliantly. Mum's had a big promotion with more money, so Dad is quitting.

He's going to college to study and retrain. He should be in heaven – lots of homework, exams and a good job at the end. One of those technology whiz-kid jobs he's always going on about, with a new Ferrari for us.

No such luck.

Listen to this . . . Dad is going to be a teacher!

And while he's at college, he's going to look after the house so Mum can concentrate on her new big job.

I've forgiven him, almost, because Mum and Dad have stopped yelling at each other. With Mum working on her papers in the lounge and Dad studying in their bedroom, our house is now so peaceful it's boring. But Connor's gran says that when you get to my age most homes seem dull and boring.

You've got to get a move on, she says, and start building your own life.

<u>For Mr Sykes. Extra English from</u>
<u>Matthew Evans</u>

I told you I could never think of
anything to write, but you said to
write about myself and my first term
at St David's.

You said it would be strictly
confidential and would never be
shown to anyone. This is just to say,
if you show this to anyone — you're
dead.

Thanks,
Matthew Evans